Black Eden

# *Cocoa*

# Baby

*An Urban Romance By:*
Shantae

www.BlackEdenPublications.com

**BLACK EDEN PUBLICATIONS™**

# *Cocoa* Baby

ISBN: 978-1523655168
United States:
10 9 8 7 6 5 4 3 2 1

# *About the Author*

Shantae is a married 35-year old mother to three teenage boys. She is an avid reader whose dream has always been to become a published author. Being a sucker for a good love story, she knew that Romance was the area she wanted to focus on with her writing while keeping a little bit of the edge Urban Lit brings. Being with her husband since she was 17 (married at 22) has provided her with plenty of experiences to share. Since her early teens, she's written poems and a few short stories but never did anything with them. For 2016, one of her resolutions was to be better about following through. Over the years, she would find herself starting a book, and just when it seemed as though she was getting somewhere, self-doubt crept in and she gave up. Shantae made a promise to herself to follow through with at least one of her book ideas, and her first novel "Cocoa Baby" was born.

"To say that I'm enjoying finally following through is an understatement. I started writing, and now, I can't seem to stop."

She is a prime example to others that it's never too late to chase your dreams. This is just the beginning!

**Facebook:** Shantae Montgomery-Knox
**Instagram:** OneDimpleTae
**Twitter:** OneDimpleTae

# Cocoa

# Baby

# *Prologue*

"I can't believe this shit is happening. How could he do this to me?" Kelsey cried out while throwing her belongings into the suitcase. She had to get the hell out of there before Shea could get home and try to explain things. There would be no talking after this because there was nothing he could say to make things better. This shit was beyond over.

Kelsey walked into the master bedroom of the home she shared with O'Shea, her boyfriend of the last seven years, and a man she had known since they were both babies. She only planned to take the things she needed. She didn't want the rest because he had purchased most of it for her. He could keep all that shit as far as she was concerned. Kelsey continued to angrily stuff more clothes into her Louis Vuitton luggage. The television was on downstairs when she vaguely heard someone mention O'Shea's name.

"What the fuck?" she said out loud.

As she rushed out, she looked over the banister down to the living area where the television was. Some celebrity entertainment show was covering the story. There was the love of her life walking side by side with some reality TV star/video vixen named Persia. Kelsey had watched that same clip at least a hundred times online since finding out. She was looking for anything in that video or in the pictures 'ol girl posted that could explain away his infidelity, but she found nothing.

*This shit can't be real life right now*, she thought.

Kelsey wasn't a hater by any means, so she could admit that the bitch he was with was pretty. From the looks of it, O'Shea wasn't expecting the paparazzi to be waiting for them when they walked out of the hotel. His face expressed total shock and regret while Persia wore a satisfied look on hers. She was enjoying every minute of this shit, and it was all at Kelsey's expense. She had never been more devastated in her life. The death of her brother was the only thing that hurt worse.

"It's not clear if Mr. Lewis has ended his relationship with longtime girlfriend and high school sweetheart Kelsey James, but if not, it's likely that she will call it quits after this," stated the reporter.

*I gotta hurry up and get the fuck up out of here*, Kelsey thought as she rushed back to the room and continued to pack.

She decided to drive back to Dallas instead of flying. She didn't want to run the risk of being recognized at the airport and have to answer any questions because she honestly didn't know what the fuck was going on herself. She needed time to think, and the three-day trip from California to Texas would give her plenty of time to do just that.

Kelsey's best friend Alana was the one who broke the news to her about O'Shea and his mistress just a few hours earlier. She had only been back in LA since yesterday and was getting things ready for him to come home from off the road. Kelsey hadn't seen him since she went to go visit her mom in Dallas a week earlier. They had gotten into a huge argument before she left about her being too busy to spend time with him when he was in town. He wanted her to travel to more away games with him or at least be available when he was home, but she was too preoccupied. She was in school to become a Nurse Practitioner and spent most of her time working or studying. O'Shea couldn't comprehend why she still wanted to work anyway. He made millions playing ball, so she didn't have to worry about anything. He just didn't understand that she wanted to be able to support herself, plus, she could never imagine letting go of her own dreams…even for him.

"You don't stop dreaming just because you got a nigga with money," she would always remind herself.

She knew he had her back and would always make sure that she was straight, but she could do that shit herself. Kelsey wasn't with O'Shea because of his money or what he could do for her. She was with him because he was her best friend and the man she wanted to be with for the rest of her life or so she thought.

In preparation for her man's return, she had been to the spa for a manicure and pedicure as well as a Brazilian bikini wax. At the salon, she had her naturally curly hair straightened, and then shopped for some super sexy lingerie at one of her favorite boutiques. She planned to make up with her baby as soon as he got home. She couldn't take it when he was mad at her because although she was being stubborn, she wanted to be with him as much as he wanted to be with her, and sometimes she let her goals and ambition get in the way of that.

*"Hey, Lana Bana," she said excited to hear from her college roommate and best friend.*

*"Hey, girl, what you up to?" Alana asked. She was surprised that her bestie was in such a good mood. It was obvious that Kelsey hadn't caught wind of what her man had been up to yet. She hated to be*

the bearer of bad news, but she wasn't about to leave her girl in the dark, looking stupid. O'Shea was her friend too, and she had known him since college, but her relationship with Kelsey trumped all that.

"Nothing much. I just made it back yesterday, and now I'm getting things ready for when my boo gets back from being on the road. What you up to?"

"Kelsey, have you talked to O'Shea today?" Alana asked not bothering to even answer her question.

"No, I haven't spoken to him since I left for Dallas. We fell out big time before I left though. Why...what's going on?"

"Have you been watching TV?" she asked.

Damn another question. What the hell was going on with this girl? Kelsey thought. "What's with all the questions, and why are you sounding like that?"

Alana always had some shit going on in her life, but little did Kelsey know, it was her life that was about to be put on front street and full of drama for a change.

"Kelsey, I need to tell you something," she started but paused trying to figure out the right words to say.

"Stop stalling, Alana. Just spit that shit out. What's going on?" she asked becoming frustrated.

"Ok, fuck it! Earlier today I was on Instagram, and I started seeing all these pictures of O'Shea popping up on my Explore page. Then I saw some of him and this chick named Persia. You may have seen her on TV before. She's on this reality show that I watch. Anyway...her and O'Shea were together...coming out of the Omni in Atlanta." She held her breath waiting on a response from her friend.

4

*"Bitch, quit playing," Kelsey laughed, totally confident that her man wouldn't play her like that, "You know Shea don't get down like that. I told you about all that social media and reality TV shit." Her man had to have a perfectly good explanation for coming out of a hotel with another female, right?*

*"Look, Kels, I didn't want to believe it at first either, but I went to this one celebrity gossip site that I go to all the time, and I saw it there too. This bitch was even taking pictures of him and posting them on her Instagram page. I know you don't want to hear this shit, but it's true. Kelsey, I know how much you love O'Shea, and I know for a fact that he loves you too. Maybe you're right though. Maybe it could all be just one big misunderstanding. I'll let you check it out for yourself."*

*Alana proceeded to give her the website info as well as Persia's IG and Twitter handles, so she could see for herself.*

*"Ok, I'll check it out and call you back," Kelsey said before hanging up the phone.*

Sure enough she found out that what Alana said was true. She couldn't believe it. Kelsey had always been secure in her relationship with O'Shea. He never gave her a reason to suspect him of stepping out on her ever. Even though he was a high-profile NBA star and the groupies were on him hard, she still trusted him with all her heart, but now all that had changed. O'Shea had been blowing her up and texting her phone for hours, so she assumed he made it home and found all her things gone. Finally blocking him, she concentrated on the long drive home. On the journey to Texas, she thought back to how it all began. She thought about the man that she had loved all of her life, and it fucked her up to think that he no longer loved her the same.

# Chapter One
## Way Back When

Kelsey had been in love with O'Shea Lewis for what seemed like forever. Because their mothers were best friends, they spent a lot of time together. Either he was at her house or she and her younger brother were at his house when their parents were working or out kicking it. Kelsey's dad had left years ago, so it was just her, her brother KJ, and her mom Anita. Ms. Vickie, O'Shea's mom, adopted him when he was just a newborn. His teenage mother was one of the many children that Vickie looked out for from time to time. O'Shea and Vickie were so close that Kelsey initially thought he was lying when he told her the story surrounding his adoption. From his relationship with his mom, she learned that you don't have to give birth to a child to be a mother to them, and Vickie was the best.

Even when Kelsey was just 14-years old, she thought O'Shea was so fine. He was 16, a grade ahead of her, and hardly paid her any attention. If anyone fucked with her, he was quick to get on their ass though. He thought of her as an annoying younger sister, but she didn't care. She felt that this young man would one day be her husband. He was everything to her, and she knew she loved him even though she wasn't exactly sure what love was. The way she felt whenever he was around had to be love though. When he would smile and his deep dimples showed, she could've melted. It was crazy that just being in his presence caused her to have the feelings she had. O'Shea had a few girlfriends over the years, and for some reason, none of them were too fond of Kelsey. However, all it took was one time for them to get out of line with her, and he would cut them loose. Around that time, he was the only boy who she was interested in, but that didn't stop other boys from showing interest in her. Every time O'Shea got wind of someone taking a liking to Kelsey, he would threaten him in one way or another to keep them away. He claimed it was because she was too young to have a boyfriend, but she had it made up in her mind that he wanted her for himself.

One night, O'Shea's mom left him in charge of her and Kelvin while she and Anita had a girls' night out. Although Kelsey didn't like the thought of having to be baby sat, she was happy just as long as she was near him. They were at the dining room table playing Spades, cracking jokes, and having a blast. That was until he started to get pissed because she was kicking his ass at the card game. It didn't help that she was talking big shit too. He taught her how to play the game, and now she stayed whopping his ass. She was talking so much trash that he decided he didn't even want to play anymore.

"Yo, I quit, man. You get on my nerves talking all that shit, lil' girl," O'Shea said standing to his feet and pushing his chair back.

"Aww, man, fuck you. You're just a sore loser, Shea," she said laughing.

"Yo' young-ass need to quit with all that cursing too," he said before storming down the hallway to his room and slamming the door behind himself.

*How could he get on my case for cursing when he curses all the time?* she thought.

O'Shea believed that there were certain things females shouldn't do. Cursing was definitely one of those things, and he reminded her of that constantly. He was so fucking bossy.

Kelsey went into the living room and noticed that her baby brother had fallen asleep watching television, so she covered him with a blanket and sat down next to him.

*How did we go from having fun to beefing?*

She hadn't meant to piss O'Shea off. She was just messing around. She hated when he was mad at her, so she got up and went down the hall to his room to apologize. "Swerve" by Lil' Boosie was blasting from the speakers of his stereo while O'Shea repeatedly shot a small basketball into a hoop he had attached to the top of his bedroom door. He was shirtless now and wore only basketball shorts and socks. Just as he was about to take another shot, his door swung open and Kelsey walked in.

"Damn, girl, you can't knock?" he asked slightly irritated.

"Nigga, I did knock…but the music is so loud you ain't hear me," she replied rolling her eyes at him. He hated when she did that shit, and she knew it.

Kelsey immediately walked over to his CDs to distract herself from staring at him with his shirt off. Acting as if she owned the place, she rapped along with Boosie and Webbie while rummaging through his stuff. O'Shea decided to ignore her and continued to shoot around. He was focused on what he was doing and was caught off guard when she came from out of nowhere and blocked a shot he threw up.

Kelsey took the ball and did her best dunk impression. They both laughed at her attempt to look like MJ with her tongue all out. After playing around for a minute, one of their favorite songs came on, and he looked up to see her prepared to do what they did every time they heard it. They both loved 90s rap music, and Lil' Kim was one of Kelsey's favorite artists. She ran over to turn up the stereo while O'Shea played the part of Lil' Cease and rapped his verse on Kim's song "Crush on You" with a pretend mic in his hand. She danced along as he did his thing and couldn't wait for her turn. After the chorus, O'Shea gave her the cue, and she went in.

"Aye, yo', shorty, won't you go get a bag of the lethal. I'll be undressed in the bra all see through. Why you count yo' jewels thinking I'ma cheat you. The only one thing I wanna do is freak you. Keep your stone sets, I got my own baguettes. And I'll be doing things that you won't regret. Lil' Kim the Queen Bee so you best take heed...shall I proceed? Yes indeed!"

O'Shea stood in place watching Kelsey as she circled around him while she rapped. He was tickled at how silly she was being. All he could do was shake his head thinking that she really thought she was the Queen B herself.

"You can slide on my ice like the escapade. And itchy-gitchy-yaya with the marmalade. Who me? Not you...oh, yes, who's he? I even dig yo' man's style, but I love yo' profile. Whisper in yo' ear and get you all shook up, but don't blush. Just keep this on the hush."

At the end of the verse, she went for it and kissed him softly on the lips. She was so caught up in the moment that she didn't realize what she was doing until it was too late. Embarrassed, she immediately started to back away from him. His facial expression was unreadable, but his eyes never left hers as she found herself being walked backward and pressed up against the wall after the brief stare down between them. O'Shea's face was so close to hers that she could feel his warm breath on her lips.

*Please kiss me!* she screamed in her head.

Her breathing and heart rate tripled, and as soon as she thought he might go for it, he put his hand on the door knob, opened the door, and shoved her out of his room. They didn't break eye contact until the door closed right in her face.

"I just came to say sorry about the game," she shouted on the other side of the door.

After she didn't get a response, she just walked away with her head down. Kelsey knew she had really messed that up and was kicking herself for doing something so stupid. His rejection hurt her feelings, but she decided not to dwell on it, and that day, she gave up on thinking that he would ever see her as anything other than a little kid. It was clear that he had never been and never would be interested in her like that.

O'Shea closed the door and he leaned against it. He didn't understand the feelings that he was having towards Kelsey, but he knew it didn't matter. She was too young for him anyway, and he chastised himself for almost kissing her back. She was like family, and his mom would kick his ass for even thinking of messing with her like that. He had plenty of chicks his age and even older who were on his dick every day, but they didn't have shit on Kelsey James though. Even at 14, she was beautiful, and he could tell that she was going to be something else when she got older. He shook it off and kept playing ball, turning the music up louder and louder, so he could get his mind off of what had just happened.

***

**Two Years Later...**

Neither Kelsey nor O'Shea discussed their kiss. They just acted as if it had never happened and went back to being like brother and sister again, but things started to change for O'Shea around the time Kelsey turned 16. She was no longer the little sister he never had. She was fine as hell, a certified dime. She had always been athletic, so her body was on point, and his favorite part of her was her fat ass. Man, it was so big and was what niggas around their way called a 'donk'. Her silky-looking skin was the color of dark chocolate, and she had long curly jet black hair. She had small round breasts, a tiny waist, and was absolutely perfect in his eyes. It wasn't just physical either. He also thought she was smart and very funny too. Her bubbly personality and sense of humor kept him laughing all the time. She had grown up nicely, and he wasn't the only guy who noticed. A bunch of dudes from school, including some of his friends, wanted the chance to talk to her, and O'Shea couldn't stand it. It took him a minute, but he would forever remember the day he finally admitted his true feelings for her. He was riding shotgun in the car with his homeboy Curtis. They were on the way to his crib to pick up some clothes so that they could go out and kick it later that night. They rolled into Curtis' apartment complex on Forest Lane bobbin' their heads to Young Jeezy's latest CD. O'Shea spotted Kelsey as soon as Curtis parked his Caprice in front of his apartment building. She was chilling with her punk-ass boyfriend Kendrick on the steps in the breezeway. She was sitting between his legs all hugged up with the nigga, and seeing that shit had O'Shea tight. Since that time she kissed him in his room two years before, she never tried again, but Lord knows he wished that she would've. He and Curtis walked up, but she was so busy all up in Kendrick's face that she didn't even notice them.

"What up, Ken?" Curtis asked.

"Nothing much, big dawg. Just chillin with my baby," he said giving him a pound and nodding 'what up' to O'Shea. O'Shea nodded back. It was no secret that the two didn't care for one another.

"Hey, Shea," Kelsey said finally acknowledging him.

"What's up?" he replied flatly.

"Dang, what's wrong with you?" She was happy to see him, but as usual, he was in a bad mood.

"Ain't nothing wrong…why?" he replied with a little more attitude than he intended.

"Because you mean mugging and shit," she snapped back.

He hadn't realized his face was screwed up until she called him out, so he tried pulling it together. That was easier said than done when it came to Kelsey though.

"Fuck you doing over here anyway? Moms know where you at?" he asked annoyed with her.

"Damn, Daddy, don't worry about it. Always up in my fucking business." Liking the sound of it, he smirked when she called him "Daddy".

"Watch your mouth, girl," he ordered still smiling a little. She didn't reply but stuck her tongue out at him before raising up to brush off the back of her jeans. O'Shea was checking her out big time, and

Kendrick peeped it, so he rose up as well and grabbed Kelsey by her hand.

"Baby, come in the crib with me real quick before you bounce," he said kissing her cheek just to fuck with O'Shea a little since he couldn't seem to keep his eyes to himself. This nigga wanted his girl, and Kendrick could tell.

Kelsey stopped straightening out her clothes and looked up at him surprised. In the three months they had been going out, she had never been inside of his home. The most they had done was kiss on his steps, so she had no idea why he wanted her to come in. They did have plans on hooking up there later after a party they were both going to, so she figured that's probably what he wanted to talk to her about. Kelsey glanced over at O'Shea who was waiting on her to answer as well, but she had no idea that his fists were balled up in his pockets and he wanted to take off on Kendrick. O'Shea was looking at her funny, but she brushed it off and turned back to Kendrick.

"Alright," she replied and began walking up the stairs behind her boyfriend. She tried her best not to look back, but when she did, she wished that she hadn't. The look on O'Shea's face let her know that he was more than just disappointed in her. He shook his head and looked away before following Curtis into his place downstairs.

Once inside the apartment that Kendrick lived in with his mother and many brothers, Kelsey asked, "So what's up? Why you want me to come up here with you?"

Without a reply, he walked up to her and began slobbing her down. The kiss was wet and sloppy, and she was completely turned off.

*Mufucka can't even kiss*, she thought.

Kendrick was good looking and slung a little shit in the hood so he stayed fresh and didn't mind spending on her. Kelsey was really trying to give him a chance, but he was making it hard as hell. She liked him enough because they did have fun when they hung out together, but he just wasn't O'Shea Lewis. For that reason alone, he could never really be the one. However, hanging out with Kendrick did take her mind off of him. Unable to take any more of the kiss, she pushed him away.

"Damn, Kendrick, what's up with you?" she asked, wiping his slobber off her face.

Surprised by her reaction, he stepped back and looked her up and down. "Ain't nothing up with me. I just wanted to be alone with you for a minute before you left especially with that nigga O'Shea staring at you like he wanna fuck or sumn'."

"Look at you acting all jealous. Don't even worry about Shea. He's like my big brother, and he just be acting overprotective…that's all," Kelsey said hoping that he hadn't picked up on her attraction to him too.

"Shit, I can't tell. Sometimes you be acting like you feeling that nigga too or sumn'. I swear he can't even ball that hard. I don't see what the hype is all about. All those bitches be on his nut sack, and he ain't even all that," he said clearly hating

"Damn, my nigga, you sound like up straight up hater," Kelsey said laughing.

"I ain't no hater. I just don't like your 'family' like that."

"Well, I think you should worry less about him and more about us," she said sweetly. She really wanted to tell the nigga that O'Shea didn't like his ass either, but she couldn't do that. She didn't want them getting into it because when it came down to it, she was *#TeamO'Shea* all day and wouldn't even hesitate to dismiss Kendrick.

"I can do that," he said pecking her on the lips, "Say, you want to go in my room for a minute?" he asked with his eyebrow raised trying to scheme on some pussy.

"Naw, you know I got to go up to the school to meet my little brother after his practice. I'm already running late as it is," she said glancing at her watch, "You still gone pick me up for the party tonight though, right?"

"Yeah, I'll be there. Did you tell your moms you were staying over your girl's house?" In his head, he was already planning to call Cherie from around the corner as soon as Kelsey left since he knew she wasn't trying to give it up. Cherie's hood rat-ass was always down to let him fuck or give him some head.

"Yeah, but I still can't stay overnight because we have an early practice at Berkner in the morning, and I'm riding up to the school with Trina."

"That's cool, boo. I'll come scoop you between 9-10 tonight. My brother should have his ass back here with my car by then."

"Ok," she replied, kissing him goodbye.

By the time Kelsey made it outside, Curtis' car was gone. She was hoping Shea wasn't mad at her still, but she knew better. She would have to hear his mouth later, and she was not looking forward to it.

*Oh, well,* she thought as she took off jogging in the direction of KJ's school.

# Chapter Two

Later that night, O'Shea and his potnahs were kicking back at a house party in the hood. O'Shea was sitting on the counter in the kitchen with some of his teammates and friends surrounding him. Everyone was drinking except for him. It just wasn't his thing, so he sipped on a bottled water instead. He wasn't trying to get caught up and make a mistake that would jeopardize his chances to play college ball and possibly in the NBA, so he didn't indulge in drinking or smoking weed like some of his friends.

"You sure you don't want a beer?" Nick, the guy who was hosting the party, asked. Nick was his friend from way back and because his folks were always out of town, he threw the best parties. O'Shea had even lost his virginity at one of Nick's older brother's parties a few years back. Nick and his brothers knew a lot of people, so in addition to his North side friends and school mates, teenagers from all over Dallas could be spotted getting their party on. It always went down when them niggas put something together, and O'Shea knew tonight would be no different. It was already packed, and the DJ had the place rocking.

"Naw, man, I'm good. You know how I do," O'Shea said, holding up his water. The boys continued to shoot the shit in the kitchen, talking about all the fine-ass girls at school, who was fucking who, and things of that nature. He knew it wouldn't be long before someone mentioned Kelsey's name. She was arguably one of the prettiest girls at their school, so she was bound to come up sooner or later.

"Say, man, that girl Kelsey is fine as hell too, and she got a big 'ol juicy booty," one of the guys said.

*Well, that didn't take long*, O'Shea thought.

"Yeah, she's like a sophomore, right?" Mike asked.

"Naw, she's a junior. I might have to see what's up with that," replied the first guy.

O'Shea was becoming irritated listening to them but didn't say anything. He didn't appreciate the way they were talking about Kelsey but couldn't trip because she wasn't his girl.

"I heard she was fucking with that nigga Kendrick though. I overheard him cappin' at school the other day talking about how he be fucking the shit out of her fine-ass," Mike said.

"Man, chill with that shit, dawg. You know she's like family to me, and I know for a fact she wouldn't even go out like that," O'Shea said checking his friend. He was unable to listen to them slander Kelsey any longer.

"Yeah, chill. Ya'll know this nigga Shea got a thing for her," Curtis teased.

"How you figure, nigga? I said she's like my little sister," he said fronting.

"Little sister my ass, nigga. Shit, I thought you was about to snatch her ass up when she was with Kendrick earlier," Curtis snickered, but he immediately threw his hands up deciding not to take his teasing any further after O'Shea shot him a dirty look. Always the jokester in the clique, everyone knew not to take anything he said to heart.

Although Curtis was speaking truth this time, O'Shea wouldn't let him know it. Honestly, he wanted to beat Kendrick's ass first, and then he would do more to her than just snatch her up.

"Real talk though, Kels is a good girl. I don't think she's fucking that nigga either," Curtis said agreeing with his boy, "And everybody knows that Kendrick has been known to lie on his dick."

Suddenly, Kelsey walked right into the kitchen, and everyone got quiet.

"What's up, fellas?" she asked smiling brightly.

She was looking good too, and even O'Shea couldn't help but stare. She had on some cut off denim shorts with a loose fitting black tank top with Tupac on the front and a red lace bra that was visible on the sides, and on her feet were a brand new pair of red, black, and white Air Max sneakers. O'Shea wanted to rip the shoes from off of her feet because she had told him a few days ago that Kendrick bought them for her. She wore her curly hair pulled up in a high ponytail with a little MAC lip gloss on her lips and nothing else. They all just stood there staring at her, not bothering to respond. Kelsey rolled her eyes at their rudeness causing her long lashes to bat as she turned to reach in the cooler for a beer having no idea that she had just been the topic of discussion.

"I know that ain't for you," O'Shea said stepping up behind her. He was actually trying to block them from getting a peek as she bent over. He knew damn well that she didn't get dressed at home because Anita would have jacked her up if she saw her wearing shorts so small that her ass was damn near hanging out of the bottoms.

"No, Pops, it's not for me. It's for Kendrick if you must know," she said rolling her eyes again.

"You came with Trina?" O'Shea asked continuing his interrogation.

"No, I rode with Kendrick. Why?"

The other guys in the kitchen looked at each other as if they were saying, "I told you so".

O'Shea peeped the looks they shot one another but ignored them. "So you gone ride home with the nigga after he been drinking?"

"Damn, Shea, one beer ain't gone kill nobody. I'm not stupid, and why you all up in my business anyway with your 'ol goody two shoes-ass?" she pouted, tired of him judging her all the time. Telling her, "Don't be out here acting like the rest of these hoes, don't do this…" or "…don't do that." She was getting sick of it. His new attitude was really starting to get on her last nerve.

"I just be trying to look out for ya' silly-ass, but you're right. Let me get up out ya' business," he spat as he brushed past her, leaving her in the kitchen with the fellas.

Cee Cee spotted him as soon as he came out and rushed over to him before anyone else could get his attention. They had hung out a few times, but they hadn't had sex yet. She was hoping to get with him tonight though. O'Shea was about to play her to the left until he saw Kelsey walk past him and over to Kendrick who was sitting on the sofa, so he wrapped his arm around Cee Cee's waist, and they started dancing to the loud music. He was trying his best to take his mind off the girl he really wanted to groove with. Kelsey noticed O'Shea when she walked out of the kitchen but ignored him and that bitch Cee Cee as she made her way over to Kendrick who was sitting on the sofa with some rat all up in his face. Once he saw Kelsey, he immediately tried to play it off like he wasn't flirting with 'ol girl, but she had already peeped the shit though. Kelsey watched him interact with the girl from the kitchen door before finally approaching them, shoving the beer toward him.

"Damn, baby, what's your problem?" Kendrick asked copping an attitude of his own for her disrespect. The girl he was talking to was still sitting too close and was looking at Kelsey like she wanted to do something. Kelsey stared the bitch down letting her know that she was definitely with the shit if she was. The girl must've gotten the picture because she quickly got up and went over to her awaiting group of friends.

*Yeah, hoe, move around before you get slid up in this bitch*, Kelsey thought, still mugging her. She wasn't trying to fight over no dude, but she wasn't about to let the girl punk her either.

"I'm ready to go," she said turning her attention back to Kendrick. O'Shea already had her in a fucked up mood and Kendrick openly flirting with other girls didn't help things either.

"We just got here. I ain't trying to leave yet. What the fuck is your problem anyway?" he asked getting fed up with Kelsey and her spoiled ways.

"My problem is that you're hella disrespectful sitting up here trying to holla at that bitch all up in my face. You think I don't know you used to talk to her. I'm not stupid Kendrick, but it's all good though. I'm leaving," she shouted, walking out the front door.

"Hold up, Kelsey," he called after her following her outside, "I'm sorry. She was trying to push up on me, but I wasn't hearing it. I wouldn't do you like that." He was lying his ass off. He had just fucked Cherie earlier that day but had no idea she was going to be at the party too. "Come on now, don't let this ruin our night. We supposed to be kicking it, remember? If you're really ready to leave, we can head on over to my crib and chill like we planned. Everybody's gone, so we will have some time alone," he smiled as he wrapped his arms around her waist. Kelsey was fine as hell, and he was willing to say whatever it took to get her back to his house tonight.

Kelsey wasn't having it though. She was never one to let a mufucka run game on her, and she knew what she saw. Kendrick was definitely kicking game to the bitch.

"Naw, my nigga, I'm good, but you can give me a ride to Trina's house though. I'm not trying to go there with you tonight. I thought about it, and I don't think I'm ready for all that just yet." He immediately released her from his embrace.

"Hell naw, Kelsey!" he raised his voice, "I'm tired of this shit. How long you expect a nigga to wait? If you ain't down, I know plenty of girls who are." He was trying to play mind games with her.

"Ok, baby," she said softly, moving to stand directly in front of him. Like a dummy, he thought that after three long months, his game had finally worked, but he found himself disappointed when she whispered in his ear, "You go on and find you one of them bitches then because I'm not the one," poking him in the chest for emphasis as she spoke.

Kelsey took off walking down the street leaving him standing there looking like a damn fool. Who the fuck did he think he was? She was not going out like that. Hell, she didn't even like the nigga enough for him to be her first anyway. She was pissed off at herself for even considering sleeping with his dog-ass because everyone knew he was a player.

*What a waste of fucking time.*

\*\*\*

O'Shea witnessed the exchange between Kendrick and Kelsey prior to them stepping outside but was determined to mind his business. That was until Kendrick returned to the party without her. He pushed Cee Cee off his lap and rushed outside to make sure she was okay, but she was nowhere to be found. He went back inside and approached Kendrick who had started back talking to the girl he was with earlier like it wasn't shit.

"Aye, my nigga, where'd Kelsey go?"

"She left, man. Why you worried about it though?" Kendrick asked. He was sick of O'Shea's cock blocking-ass.

"Fuck all that shit you kicking. Didn't she ride here with you?" O'Shea asked ready to go off.

Kendrick was getting more annoyed by the second. "Yeah, she did, but she decided she was ready to leave, but as you can see, my nigga, I'm not. You can go find her if you want. I already got what I wanted from her anyway," he smirked.

O'Shea wanted to punch Kendrick in his face but decided to focus on finding Kelsey. He would have to deal with this fool another time. Cee Cee attempted to block him from going after her, but he shut her down, telling her he would get with her tomorrow. He drove around the neighborhood for a few minutes before he spotted Kelsey walking down Audelia.

*She knows damn well it's not safe for her to be walking around here at this time of night by herself,* he thought as he pulled up alongside her and rolled down the window.

"Kelsey get in and let me take you home." He was pissed, but he'd be damned if he let anything happen to her.

"No, Shea, I'm good. I just want to be alone right now," she replied not bothering to look his way.

"Girl, get yo' ass in this car. You know I'm not about to let you walk home in this neighborhood this late."

She thought about it and realized he was right. She had already been approached by a group of guys yelling inappropriate things to her near the convenience store. Thinking of what could happen to her out there all alone, she decided to accept the ride.

They rode in silence for a few minutes before O'Shea spoke. "You okay?"

"Yeah, I'm good," Kelsey replied still looking out of the window.

"You hungry? I was about to head to *Jack-in-the-Box* to get something to eat," he said knowing some food would cheer her greedy-ass up.

"Hell yeah, you know that's my shit," she said smiling and feeling better already. He just shook his head and laughed.

After ordering their food in the drive-thru, they sat in the car and ate. They laughed and talked while they devoured their burgers and fries, silently squashing the beef between them earlier. O'Shea informed her that he had decided to attend Baylor University next fall on a full basketball scholarship.

"Congratulations, I'm so proud of you, Shea." Kelsey was excited for him because she knew how much playing basketball meant to him, but she would miss having him around though.

"Thanks, Cocoa," he said smiling as he pulled out of the parking lot.

"Ugh! Stop calling me that," she said annoyed while he just laughed it off.

After a few minutes she noticed that they were going towards her house. "Hey, I'm not going home. I lied and told mama I was staying at Trina's house tonight."

"Why would you do that Kelsey?" he asked, hoping she wouldn't say what he was thinking.

"Because I was planning on going home with Kendrick," she replied with her head down. Kelsey didn't want him to look down on her. Even though she wouldn't admit it, his opinion mattered a lot to her.

His jaw clenched at her response. "So it's true...you fucking that nigga?" he asked glaring at her.

Shocked by his reaction, her head shot up and her eyes widened. She couldn't believe he was acting like he was pissed off. She didn't know what was going on with him, but he had been acting real funny lately.

"No, we ain't fucking, Shea," she replied, rolling her eyes, "I was thinking maybe tonight would be the night, but I'm glad I didn't go through with it."

Softening a little, he replied, "I'm glad too," but he didn't mean to say that out loud. "Anyway, you can crash at the house, or I can take you back to Trina's. Ma is working tonight, but you know she wouldn't mind. Shit, ya'll always at the house anyway."

"I'll just go to the house with you. Trina's brother James always tries to get at me, and I don't feel like fighting that nigga off tonight," she said happy she didn't have to stay at her friend's. They kept a nasty house, and she knew she wouldn't get much sleep for fear of a roach ending up in her ear or mouth. She hated that she slept with her mouth open.

"Cool," he replied, turning the car around and heading to his house.

"Can I ask you something, Shea?"

"Yeah, what's up?"

"Why did you say you were glad that me and Ken didn't do anything tonight?"

"Because I think you deserve better," he replied truthfully. He really thought she deserved him, but he couldn't tell her that.

"You're right, Shea. I think I do too," she replied with a cute smirk.

He looked away and tried to focus on driving.

*Why does she have to be so damn cute?*

O'Shea was feeling different about her, and he couldn't describe it, but it was a feeling he'd never had before. If he was honest with himself, he would admit that he always had a crush on her but tried to downplay it because she was a little younger and they were like family, so that's how he treated her, like a little sister. Now things were changing, and he was starting to see her as someone he wanted to be with.

\*\*\*

Back at the house, they chilled in the living room and watched her favorite DVD *You So Crazy*. She was laughing and quoting Martin line for line. Her little brother hated when she did that shit, but O'Shea didn't mind at all. She was so animated that she had him laughing more at her than at Martin. He didn't realize that he was staring at her until she looked over at him, but it was too late to turn away.

"What?" she asked noticing something different in his eyes. It caused her heart to beat faster and her palms to sweat.

"I don't know. I just think you're beautiful," he replied honestly while maintaining eye contact with her.

Kelsey was surprised by his response. "Since when, Shea?" she asked with her lips turned up, not really believing him.

"Since forever, Kelsey," he said as he continued to stare.

She didn't know he looked at her that way, and his revelation made her panties get wet immediately. They didn't speak for a few moments and seemed to be communicating with each other with only their eyes. Kelsey stood up first, and O'Shea followed suit, moving into her personal space. She grabbed his arms and placed them around her waist, and before she knew it, he leaned down and kissed her like he'd wanted to do since the first time she kissed him. Kelsey took his breath away when she moaned into his mouth and deepened the kiss even more. The kiss was everything, better than either of them had ever dreamed of. He never wanted it to stop. His hands moved from her waist to her round ass, and he gripped it like he had in his fantasies about her. Kelsey stood on her tip toes returning the kiss with as much passion as him.

"Damn," he said, finally breaking away. He felt like his heart was beating out of his chest, and his dick was rock hard. "We gotta chill, Cocoa," he said trying to catch his breath, "If you keep kissing me like that, I won't be able to stop."

"I don't want you to stop," she replied dead serious as she licked her lips trying to taste him some more.

"You ain't ready for that," he said, recalling their conversation regarding her sleeping with Kendrick. He didn't want to rush her into something she wasn't ready for. He wanted her bad, but if they did hook up, it would be on her terms.

Kelsey boldly reached down and stroked him through his Levis causing him to gasp and grow another inch from her touch. "I wasn't ready with him, but I am with you," she whispered.

Her words sparked something deep down within him. He caressed the sides of her face and kissed her again. The kiss was more intense this time as they both realized what was about to go down. They had waited and denied their true feelings for one another for far too long. O'Shea cupped her ass once more, and she wrapped her arms around his neck. Kelsey felt like she was going to explode from his kisses alone. Crazy sensations had her going bananas on the inside, and she couldn't wait any longer. O'Shea picked her up, and she immediately wrapped her legs around his waist. They didn't break the kiss as he walked with her in his arms down the hallway to his bedroom. Once inside, he laid her down on his bed and proceeded to undress all the way down to his boxers. Seeing his dick print caused her to smile and bite her top lip. She hurried to remove her own clothes, but he stopped her.

"No, let me," he said removing her shorts first. Kelsey was wearing a cute pair of lace bikini panties. She smelled so sweet that it made him want to know how she tasted. He had never gone down on a girl before, but he knew for a fact that he wanted to taste her tonight, so he removed her panties, and she sat up to assist him as he removed her shirt. O'Shea kissed her again and reached around to unfasten her matching lace bra. He stopped kissing her and took one of her perky breasts into his mouth, thinking even they tasted good. They were small but just enough for him.

*Perfect*, he thought, as he fell in love with her body inch by inch.

She was moaning, and the sounds she made urged him to continue. He showed love to her other breast, and by then, she was gripping the sheets and squirming. He relished the fact that he was making her feel this way. Finally reaching his destination, he began licking and sucking on her peach. He had no idea what he was doing but figured he must have been doing it right because she was going wild especially when he repeatedly flicked his tongue against her clit. Delicious was the only word that came to mind when he tasted her first orgasm. He knew that from that day forward, he would be addicted to her scent, her taste, and everything else about her chocolate-ass.

Kelsey's first orgasm from having him go down on her was something she would never forget. Nothing had ever felt so good, and after the second one washed over her, she had to have him.

"Shea, please give it to me," she begged. Her moans and pleading drove him crazy. He donned a condom he grabbed from off the nightstand and opened her legs wide using his knee. The head of his dick was at her entrance, and he moved it up and down her wetness. She humped the air silently begging for the dick with her eyes closed tight.

"Open your eyes, Kelsey. I need you here with me. I gotta know that you really wanna do this. I promise you I don't mind waiting."

She opened her eyes, and they were pleading with him to continue. He had his answer. She didn't want to wait. She wanted him as much as he wanted her, so he entered her slowly, only giving her half at first. She tensed up and gasped at the feel of him easing inside. It hurt like hell, but she wanted to feel all of him.

"Please, don't stop," she whined. She was so tight, and he had never felt anything like it. Everything about this moment felt right. He was met with resistance and was about to pull out again, but she placed her hands on his ass and forced him all the way into her. The pain she felt was intense but brief.

"Awww shit!" he called out, surprised by her aggression. The shit felt amazing. He'd had sex a few times before, but this shit was crazy especially once she got used to his size.

Kelsey caught her rhythm and began working her hips. O'Shea didn't think he could take much more but didn't want to bust too fast.

*Stay focused*, he coached himself.

He was so excited to be her first, and he knew that he wanted to be with her from that moment on. He actually knew he wanted to be with her before they had sex, but that night confirmed it for him. He didn't want her to be with anyone else.

*She's mines*, he kept repeating in his head.

"You're mine, Kelsey! You're all mine," he moaned sliding in and out of her.

He hadn't realized he was speaking out loud until she repeated the words he spoke. "I'm all yours, baby," she whispered.

He opened his eyes to find her looking up at him. He reached under her and gripped her ass bringing her up to meet his strokes and go even deeper. She wrapped her legs around him and threw her arms around his neck as their lips reunited for another kiss. He felt his orgasm building, and she was on her way to a third. He came so hard that he couldn't see straight for a full minute. He thought he had gone blind. They were both out of breath, and it took all his strength to pull out and move to lay down beside her. They just laid there gazing at one another, having no regrets about what they had just done. He kissed her sweetly causing her to want to be closer to him. She climbed over and rested her body on top of his. Her head was on his chest, and she could hear his heart beating fast, matching the rhythm of her own. Before she knew it, they drifted off into a peaceful slumber.

# Chapter Three

O'Shea woke up after a couple hours and headed to the restroom attached to his bedroom to throw away the condom he had just finished using and clean himself up. When he returned to the bed, he watched as Kelsey slept, admiring her naked body. She was a dark chocolate beauty, and he absolutely loved every inch of her unblemished cocoa-colored skin—his *Cocoa Baby*. He went into the living room to collect her belongings and brought them into his room thinking that he locked his bedroom door behind him. O'Shea didn't want his mother to come home and find a girl in his bed especially since the girl was Kelsey. If she came home, and Kelsey was asleep on the couch that would be different and something that was common, but if she found her in his bed, Vickie would fuck him up for sure. Once he finished, he rejoined Kelsey, wrapping his arm around her waist after setting the alarm clock for *6:30 a.m.* The plan was to wake up before his mom got off work and take Kelsey to her friend Trina's house, but for now, all he wanted to do was enjoy being there with her.

Hours later, he woke up with the morning sunlight shining through his window.

*What time is it?* he thought, reaching for the clock.

It was after 8 a.m., but he hadn't heard the alarm go off, and Kelsey was still asleep with her head resting on his chest. He kissed the top of her head attempting to wake her.

"Kelsey, wake up."

She raised her head and smiled up at him with one eye open. "What time is it?" she asked still half-sleep.

"It's almost 8:15 a.m.," he replied.

She jumped up. "Fuck, I gotta get to practice." Her expression turned fearful when she thought of another problem they had. "Is Ms. Vickie here?" she asked nervously looking around for her clothes.

"Don't even trip. She probably came home, took a shower, and went straight to bed. Come on, so I can get you to Trina's before you miss practice."

"Ok, cool, let me wash up real quick," she said as she picked up her belongings that he placed on the chair near his computer.

O'Shea watched her until she disappeared behind the bathroom door. He hurried to get dressed as he tried to straighten up his room. While he was making the bed, he noticed blood on his sheets. He just smiled and shook his head remembering what they had shared the night before. After Kelsey finished up in the restroom, they quietly made their way through the house and out to his car, clueless that they were being watched the entire time. O'Shea grabbed Kelsey's hand and held it on the drive over to Trina's house. He was feeling her more than ever, and last night sealed the deal for him. O'Shea hoped she felt the same way because he definitely wanted to be her nigga.

*Where do we go from here? Was this just a one-time thing? Does he really want to be with me, or was he just trying to fuck? He said I was his, but niggas probably say a bunch of shit when they're knee-deep in some pussy.* Kelsey had a million things on her brain at that moment because there were so many questions she didn't have the answers to.

O'Shea parked his car a few houses down from Trina's so that no one would see her getting out.

"Kelsey, about last night," he started. She was already dreading what he was about to say next and could already feel her heart breaking. He looked at her strangely before continuing. "You're wrong," he said shaking his head at her.

"What you mean I'm wrong?" she asked totally confused.

"For what you're thinking right now. You think I regret what happened last night, but I don't. If you think it was just a 'hit it and quit it' thing for me, then you're wrong. I meant what I said."

"And what's that?" she asked already knowing, but she still needed to hear him say it.

"You're mine, and I want to be with you," he replied, dead-ass serious.

"I want to be with you too," she grinned totally relieved.

"I'm serious, Kelsey. I don't want you with nobody else so dead that shit with Kendrick. I would hate to have to beat his ass behind you, but I will. I already want to fuck him up for that shit he pulled last night."

"I'll handle it, Shea, and don't worry about Kendrick. I only want you. I always have," she said.

Her admission made him blush a little. "Ok, then, I'll let you handle it. I'm gon' get up with you later then, Cocoa Baby," he said licking his lips.

She rolled her eyes at the mention of his nickname for her and moved toward the door to exit the car, but he grabbed her arm to stop her. Leaning over, he kissed her, and she wondered if she would feel this way every time they kissed. Each time their lips met, she felt a sensation that fluttered in her chest, quivered down through her stomach, and pounded between her legs. It felt so good that she just knew she could experience an orgasm from his kisses alone. When he finally released her, she got out and jogged up the street to Trina's hoping she didn't make everyone late.

***

Back at the house, O'Shea rushed to his room wanting to clean up a little more before his mother had a chance to do it. She had a habit of picking up after him, but when he opened the door to his room, he realized it was too late. His room was already clean and his bed had been stripped of all the bedding. He was scared as hell as he walked across the hall to Vickie's room and gently knocked on her door with a shaky hand. She had to have known that he had someone over last night from the blood on his sheets, and he was not looking forward to this conversation.

"Come on in, boy," she said sitting on the edge of her bed waiting for him.

"Hey, Ma, how was work?" he asked trying to play it cool.

"Have a seat, son," she said pointing toward the lounge chair across from her bed. He did as he was told, letting his head fall to his chest prepared for her to go in on him.

"You know every morning when I get home from a long night at the hospital, I have a routine. I take off my shoes in the garage before I go to the kitchen to fix me a light snack, but before I go to my room to take a shower and lay down, I always peep in on my one and only baby boy."

Her statement caused him to raise his head. *The fuck? I know I locked my door, didn't I?* He wanted to speak up and say something but nothing came out. This was bad; this was all bad.

"Imagine my surprise when I opened your door to see you and Kelsey laid up in the bed like ya'll grown and paying bills up in this bitch," she said with her head cocked to the side.

"Ma, I'm sorry. I'm so sorry. Last night was the first time me and Kelsey ever did anything like that." He lowered his head again, hating to disappoint his mother. "But I take full responsibility for what happened. Please don't be mad at Kelsey, Ma. I really care about her, and this wasn't something we planned. It just happened…," he rambled on.

"Son, I'm not mad at either of you. Shocked by what I saw? Yes, but mad? No. I know how you feel about Kelsey, the way you two feel about each other. I don't have an issue with you and Kels being together, Shea, but you need to be careful, baby. You don't want to make a mistake and end up getting her pregnant. She has goals for her life, and so do you. A baby could put all that on pause. You understand what I'm saying, boy?"

"Ma, we used protection," he replied.

"O'Shea Lewis, we have had this conversation before. Condoms are not 100%. Things happen all the time, and I want you to be responsible with Kelsey's body as well as her heart. She is like a daughter to me, and I want the best for the both of you. I would rather you two have waited to have sex, but at this point, all I can do is tell you to be safe."

"I hear you, Ma."

"One more thing," she said as he rose from the chair thinking they were done talking.

"Yes, ma'am," he replied.

"If you ever disrespect me like that in my house again, I will put my foot up your 6'3, red, narrow-ass. Do you understand me?" she asked. He knew she was playing no games.

"I'm sorry, Ma, and it won't happen again. By the way, I'm 6'5 now," he smiled.

"I don't give a damn, Shea. I'll still beat yo' tall-ass," she laughed, "Now get on out, so I can get some rest." As much as she wanted to be mad, all she could do was shake her head at her son.

"Ok, Ma, love you," he said before kissing her on the cheek and leaving her room.

"I love you too, baby."

O'Shea jumped in the shower after putting clean linen on his bed. He decided to go watch Kelsey practice at Berkner. It was crazy how they were just into it yesterday, and now they were in a relationship, but he wouldn't have had it any other way though. When O'Shea pulled up to the school, he saw Kendrick's Crown Vic parked out front. He spotted him up in the bleachers surrounded by a few chicks from their school watching Kelsey run too. O'Shea beamed with pride as his girl finished in first place. She was a beast at the hurdles, but she loved running long distance. He ran with her sometimes, but her ass never wanted to stop, running ten or more miles at a time. He was in great shape as well. He had to be for basketball, "but fuck all that. Ain't nobody trying to run no ten miles," he would always tell her.

Because Kelsey was so focused, she didn't even notice O'Shea until practice was over. As she was gathering her belongings, she happened to glance up and noticed him looking her way. She stared at him thinking he was fine as hell. O'Shea was tall with an athletic build, fair-skinned with beautiful eyes, and the deepest dimples she'd ever seen. She smiled brightly walking over to where he was not even seeing Kendrick sitting about four rows above him. Kendrick stood up about the same time she reached O'Shea. He was hoping she was coming over to speak to him and that she was no longer pissed at him for what had gone down the night before, but he got the shock of his life as he watched her climb the bleachers and stop in front of O'Shea, standing in between his legs.

"I didn't know you were coming," she smiled.

"I guess I was missing you already, and I wanted to see you. You riding with me?" he asked grabbing her hand.

"Hell yeah, I'm riding with you," she replied as he stood up towering over her small 5'5 frame. He pulled her close and kissed her just like he'd been thinking of doing since he dropped her off earlier. The fact that Kendrick was a witness was just a bonus.

Suddenly, becoming self-conscious, she pulled back. "Ewww, Shea, I'm all sweaty and funky."

"Girl, I don't give a fuck about none of that," he replied kissing her all over her damp face. Kelsey could definitely get used to the affectionate side of O'Shea.

"I guess I was right, huh, Kelsey?" Kendrick shouted with an attitude, clearly mad about what he saw. He was thinking that she had been playing him for this nigga the whole time. *Big brother my ass*, he thought.

She looked up shocked to see him standing there. She was thinking he sure had a lot of nerve acting like he was mad after the way he did her last night. She looked to O'Shea, and he was giving her a look that said, "You better let this nigga know what's up," so Kelsey turned back to Kendrick smiling.

"I guess you were," she replied, walking off hand in hand with Shea.

***

After stopping by Trina's to take a quick shower and pick up her stuff, Kelsey and O'Shea spent the rest of the day hanging out. He dropped her off at home that evening around 9 p.m. They both wanted to have sex, but she told him she wanted to wait until she got on some birth control, and reluctantly he agreed. When she did finally make it home, she was met at the door by her mother, and she was not a happy camper.

"Kelsey Marie James, where the hell have you been? You left here yesterday going to Trina's, and you just now showing back up? I don't know what you think this is, but you ain't grown or too old to get your ass whooped," her mother fussed.

"My bad, Mama. I told you I had practice this morning, and afterwards I was kicking it with Shea."

"'My bad my ass. Running around Dallas like you grown and not even bothering to check in. Don't do that shit again, Kelsey, and what you doing hanging out with O'Shea all day for anyway?"

"It ain't nothing, Mama. We hang out sometimes…you know that," she said on the way to her room with Anita following close behind. She apologized for not checking in again and again, and they ended up talking for about ten minutes before she went back into the den to watch television.

Kelsey went to run herself a bath, adding Epsom salt and bubbles. Her body was still sore from the activities from the night before and practice that morning. While the tub filled with water, she went down the hall to check on her little brother Kelvin Jr. She knocked and opened the door after he said it was okay come in.

"Hey, baby bro, what you up to?" she asked sitting at the foot of his bed while he sat on the floor playing his game.

"Not shit. Where you been?"

"Practice," she said, popping him on his head, "Watch your mouth."

Kelsey knew she needed to be a better influence on her brother. He was picking up some of her bad habits, and she couldn't have that. She loved this little dude more than life itself and couldn't believe what a big boy he was now. At 12-years old, he was a very handsome young man with the same chocolate-skin tone as hers. He was also extremely smart, and unlike a majority of siblings, the two of them were close and rarely ever fought.

"My bad, sis, you want to play *2K* with me?" he asked.

"Yeah, I'll get on it with you when I get out of the tub," she promised.

After making sure the water was just right, Kelsey slid right in, but she didn't realize how sore she really was until her skin hit the hot soapy water. Her limbs were super tight, and her entire body felt worn out. Who would have thought that she and O'Shea would ever hook up? Being with him was something she'd wanted for a long time, and the sex, my goodness, it was so good. She was geeked that he was her first. Good thing Kendrick fucked things up because sleeping with him would have been a huge mistake. Kelsey couldn't wait to see Shea again. They planned to link up the following day and catch a movie. She needed to talk to her mother about getting on birth control soon. Now that she had been intimate with Shea, she knew she wanted to do it again and again, but she couldn't get caught up with a baby though. She had big dreams, and so did he.

# Chapter Four

Even after staying on the phone with Shea until around three o'clock in the morning, Kelsey was still up early Sunday morning to prepare breakfast for her family. She enjoyed eating and clowning with KJ while her mother slept in. They planned to go to New Mt. Zion for the late service. KJ was leaving the table at the same time their mother walked into the kitchen. Kelsey figured this would be the perfect time to talk to her about a few things. Even though she and her mom were close, Kelsey was still nervous to tell her about having sex with Shea. Her mother loved O'Shea like a son, so it wasn't so much about him. This just wasn't an easy subject to discuss with your parents; however, it was necessary that she let her mother know what was going on and how she was feeling.

"Well, you haven't done this in a minute, Miss Kelsey," her mother pointed out.

"I know, Mama, I just wanted to do something special for you. Let me fix you a plate," she said.

*Here it goes*, her mother thought to herself.

Anita knew her daughter well, and she'd definitely noticed something different about her yesterday, but she decided not to bring it up. They had always had a close relationship, so she knew that whatever was going on with her baby, she would come to her when she was ready to talk about it. They had an open line of communication and had always been able to talk about anything.

*Look at her, she's even walking different*, Anita thought as she watched Kelsey move around the kitchen.

"How has work been going?" she asked, stalling a little.

"Kelsey, cut this shit out and talk to me, baby. What's going on?" Anita asked ready to get this conversation over with.

"Ok, Mama, you got me," she laughed, "You remember when we talked about me getting on birth control when I was ready to have sex, right?"

"Yes, I remember, child, but I also remember you telling me that you weren't ready and wouldn't be for a while," Anita said recalling the conversation they had the year before.

"Well, at the time I wasn't ready, but I am now and…I want to get on the pill," she blurted out.

"First of all, what makes you so sure you're ready? And secondly, are you thinking about having sex or have you already had sex, Kelsey?"

Although, she already knew the answer, she wanted to hear it from her. Now that the time had come, Anita wasn't so sure that she was ready for her daughter to grow up on her. She was a teenage mother and not long after her second child was born, her husband was long gone in the streets and strung out on drugs. She didn't want her daughter to make the same mistakes she had, and even though she still managed to put herself through school while working full-time, it wasn't easy.

Kelsey took a deep breath and replied, "I already had sex...for the first time last night."

Anita was aware that her daughter had a little boyfriend, but she didn't really didn't care for him too much. He had 'dope boy' written all over him, and she didn't want Kelsey associated with that type of mess.

"With Kendrick?!"

"Naw, Mama, I broke up with him…it was with Shea," she replied. Kelsey braced herself, waiting for her mother's reaction.

"Lord Jesus! So you and O'Shea finally admitted to liking each other, huh?" Anita's response shocked Kelsey.

"What are you talking about?" she asked.

"Child, I've been knowing how you felt about O'Shea. Since you were a little girl, you have had the biggest crush on him, and he might not admit it, but he's always liked you too and has always been very protective of you. Vickie and I knew one day you two would eventually start dating. I guess ya'll decided to stop fighting the inevitable."

"I guess we did," she smiled, "It's so crazy because all we do is argue, and I had no idea that he even saw me that way."

"Seems like you were the only one who couldn't see it."

Kelsey had always been aware of how she felt about O'Shea but was clueless when it came to how he really felt about her.

"Well, we're together now, and I just want us to be responsible, so that's why I want to get on the pill."

"I know you do, and I am proud of you for doing the right thing and coming to talk to me about it. It's easy to have slips ups with protection or become careless when you're in love like that and I'm not telling you what I heard, I'm telling you what I know."

Anita knew her daughter had deep feelings for O'Shea, and their relationship reminded her of her and her husband Kelvin's when they first started out. She still missed his ass like crazy. He was the only man she had ever loved. She had a few "special" male friends over the years, but no one compared to Kelvin Wayne James.

"I'll set up your appointment first thing in the morning," she said not wanting to continue reminiscing about her estranged husband.

"Thanks, Mama. I love you."

"I love you too, baby. Now let's hurry and get dressed for church before we're late," Anita said finishing off the rest of her food.

***

From that point on, Kelsey and O'Shea were inseparable, but the couple didn't have sex again until she was on birth control. Kelsey was playing no games when it came to that, and he loved that about her. Their love for one another grew, and O'Shea planned to one day make her his wife. Although, he went off to Baylor for college the following year, they made the long distance thing work. She visited him at school often, and he came home to see her in Dallas as much as possible. She never worried about him and other females because he made her feel like she was the only one for him. He respected her, and she trusted him completely.

Senior year in high school was one of the hardest times of Kelsey's life. For one, she missed O'Shea like crazy, and it was also the year that she lost her brother Kelvin Jr. He was riding in the car with some much older friends when they were hit by a drunk driver. There were three boys in the car, but Kelvin was the only one who succumbed to his injuries. The other two teenagers walked away with a few minor cuts and scrapes. O'Shea drove home from school as soon as he found out, and if it was not for him, Kelsey would have lost her mind. Shea and Kelvin were close as well, so he took his death hard but was trying to be strong for his girl. He held her in his arms all night as she cried uncontrollably and repeated, "My baby is gone, Shea" in between sobs. It hurt him to see her in that condition, but he had to remind her that her mother was also having a hard time and she needed to get it together so that she could be there for her. Kelsey knew he was right. She was so lost in her own grief that she had forgotten all about her poor mother. She had lost her only son, and Kelsey couldn't even imagine what that felt like. At the funeral, she half-expected to see her father, but he didn't have the guts to show up, and she hated him for that. It pissed her off that her mother had to bury her only son, and this nigga wasn't man enough to show up and support her. Everyone from her father's side of the family was there, so there was no way he couldn't have known what happened to KJ.

Kelsey joined O'Shea at Baylor University the following year where she would eventually receive a Bachelor of Science in Nursing following in both of their mother's footsteps. The groupies were on O'Shea tough, but it was no different from when they were in high school. Kelsey wasn't stuntin' them hoes because he curved them left and right just like he had done back home. She was all he needed, and he made sure she knew it too. It wasn't like dudes didn't flock to her as well. She was beautiful, smart, outgoing, and just fun to be around. She knew she had it going on, but she didn't pay the guys who came at her any mind because she only had eyes for Shea, plus, she knew better. Her man was crazy as hell. He took off on a nigga at a party off campus one night for trying to holla at her. It wasn't so much that the dude was trying to talk to her but the fact that he started tripping after she politely turned him down was what made him snap. O'Shea beat dude's ass after he grabbed Kelsey by the arm and began calling her all kinds of "stuck up bitches" amongst other foul names. There was no calming him, and she was scared of what he would do because she had never seen him so angry. He told her when he saw 'ol boy all in her face grabbing her and disrespecting her, he blacked out.

Later he told her, "You're going to be my wife one day, and I can't have niggas around here putting their hands on you. I don't do that shit to you, so what I look like letting some other nigga get away with it? These hands will only be used to make you feel good, not to hurt you, you feel me?" Yes, she felt him, and she loved when his large hands caressed her body. His hands definitely made her feel good.

O'Shea made a promise to his mother and to Kelsey that he would remain in college to receive his degree before entering the draft. A few of his teammates left after their sophomore year for the NBA, but he decided against it. After he received his degree, he entered the draft, and was picked up by LA in the 2nd round. Kelsey remained at Baylor to finish up her last year. They had done the long distance thing before and felt they could survive one more year apart, so they traveled back and forth to spend as much time together as they could. As far as O'Shea was concerned, she couldn't graduate quickly enough. He was enjoying playing basketball and the money he was making, but he was ready to have his woman with him permanently. After graduation, Kelsey moved to LA with O'Shea and immediately enrolled into school with hopes of becoming a Nurse Practitioner. O'Shea didn't like the idea and felt that she could have waited a little while before starting. He felt they had been apart for long enough, and he just wanted her to himself for a little while before she threw herself into work and books again. She wasn't trying to hear it though. He wanted to get married and start a family right away, but she wanted to hold off until she completed her education. She was looking forward to being done and focusing more on her relationship. She wanted to get married and have O'Shea's babies too, but she just wanted to accomplish her goals first. Plus, she wanted to travel and live a little before they tied themselves down with children. He would be on the road a lot, so she was the one who would be at home with the kids...not him. It wasn't that she would mind it, but she felt that she needed more time with just the two of them. She usually went along with whatever O'Shea said just to keep him happy, but this was something she wouldn't budge on, and he had no understanding. At first, she made a huge effort to spend time with him. Kelsey wanted to reassure him that he was still number one in her life. She tried to make as many away games as she could and attended every single home game. If she wasn't there, she knew he would have a fit. Her grades began to slip because she wasn't spending enough time studying, so she had to buckle down if she was going to graduate in the timeframe she set for herself. To make matters worse, she was also working full-time. They constantly went back and forth about it. They had never argued this much before, and it was taking a toll on them both. It seemed like they were moving in two different directions, and it scared the hell out of them. More and more, Kelsey began missing games and spending less time with O'Shea. She could tell they were growing apart. That's why she came back from Dallas to LA early. She began to realize that she was letting school and work interfere with their relationship. She didn't have to work; she chose to work. She didn't have to go to school full-time, but she chose to so that she could get done quicker, but Kelsey was beginning to see it was all at the expense of her relationship though, so she decided to go part-time at work and take some time off from school. She couldn't lose O'Shea because he meant the world to her, and she planned to let him know that as soon as he made it home. She never got the chance to make things right though. Her whole world came crashing down around her when she arrived back in LA. She'd lost her best friend and the love of her life all at the same damn time. She didn't want to believe it was over between them, but she knew that she couldn't be with him after that.

*Where the hell do I go from here?* she thought on her way back to Texas with tears streaming down her face.

# Chapter Five
*Here and Now*

***Two Years Later...***

When Kelsey was done packing, she picked up her phone from the nightstand to call her mother.

"Well, hello, Miss Kelsey."

"Hello, Bernice," she said smiling.

"What the hell I tell you about calling me 'Bernice'?" Anita asked trying her best to sound irritated.

"I call you Bernice because you act like an old-ass lady, and Bernice is definitely an old-ass lady name," she laughed. Her mom couldn't help but laugh too. "I'm just playing with you, Mom. I just wanted to check in with you before I left. My flight leaves at 12:50 p.m. I'll call you after I make it and get settled in."

"Ok, baby girl, I hope you have a great time," she said unable to mask the concern in her voice.

Sensing her mother's anxiety about her traveling on her own, Kelsey reassured her that she would be fine.

"Mom, I'll be fine, and I'll call you often to let you know how things are going," she promised.

"I know, baby. I just worry about you. You're all I have left," Anita said sadly.

"I'll be fine, Mama. Please don't worry," Kelsey said attempting to calm her mother's nerves.

"I know you will, baby. Now you go on to Jamaica and have a fabulous time. You have worked very hard the last few years and deserve this time off. Let me get off this phone so I can be dressed before Vickie pulls up and curses me out for not being ready."

Kelsey laughed. "Now where are you and Ms. Vickie going?"

"We're going to brunch at Gloria's, do a little shopping, and then go play bingo."

"See, I told you. That's that old lady shit. Going to play bingo, huh?"

"Forget you, Kelsey," Anita laughed, "O'Shea just got her a new Lexus, and she wants me to be her riding partner today."

"That was nice of him," she replied flatly.

"You know he was asking about you when he called me for my birthday, and before you say anything, I know you don't want to talk about it, smart-ass."

Her mother knew her all too well and knew what her response would be anytime the subject of O'Shea came up.

"You're right, Mom. I don't want to talk about it. Anyway, I still have a few things to do and I don't want to miss my flight. I love you. You and Ms. Vickie have a good time today. Make sure you tell her I love and miss her."

"Will do, baby, and I love you too."

Kelsey ended the call with her mom and finished up some last minute chores. She and Anita were very close and became even closer after the death of her brother. Anita and Kelsey's father Kelvin were madly in love as teenagers but parted ways soon after the birth of KJ due to his addiction to crack cocaine. It had been years since Kelsey had seen or heard from her father. She did remember him as a loving and caring man though. She often had flashbacks of times before their family was torn apart. They used to have family outings to the park or the movies, but what stood out most in her mind was the love her parents had for one another. The way they touched and looked at each other when they thought no one was watching was something to see. Kelsey thought she had found that same love with O'Shea, but she was wrong.

Kelsey was excited and looking forward to some fun in the sun. Romelo, her new friend, wanted her to postpone her vacation by two weeks, so that he could accompany her on the trip, but she was like, "Hell no." She scheduled it this week because she knew he would be too busy to go. He was set to speak at a few medical conferences at the hospital where they met and both worked. He was a surgeon in the General Surgery Department, and she was a Registered Nurse in the ICU. They had been seeing each other for about nine months now, but they had an understanding. He knew she didn't want a serious relationship, just some fire sex and maybe an outing here and there. He was totally on board in the beginning, stating that he too wasn't looking for a committed relationship, but a few months in, he started to change his tune. These days, Melo was becoming clingy, calling her all the time and practically demanding that she change the plans for her trip to include him. Kelsey knew she definitely had to end things with him when she returned home from Jamaica. She didn't know what he thought was going on, but love didn't live there no more. It was a shame too because Romelo Harris was gorgeous, successful, and his sex game was out of this world. It wasn't his fault that Kelsey had given her heart away a long time ago and had yet to receive it back.

***

It was Kelsey's second day in Jamaica, and she was enjoying herself so far. It was the beginning of June, and the weather was perfect. She had just showered and applied Aveeno lotion all over her smooth cocoa skin. After dressing, she admired herself in the mirror. She wore a multicolored Maxi dress that was perfect for her tiny waist and perfectly round behind. She wasn't as blessed in the breast department, but she was cool with that. She had a mouthful, so she wasn't tripping. She worked out regularly and ran more than twenty miles per week, so she was in excellent shape. She accessorized accordingly and finished off her look with a cute pair of Christian Dior sandals that she purchased before coming there. She had also treated herself to a full spa day prior to the trip. Her eyebrows were neatly threaded, her entire body freshly waxed, and her mani-pedi was on point. Kelsey looked great and felt even better.

Never having had a perm, Kelsey wore her hair natural before it became the cool thing to do. She deep conditioned her hair the night before and did two strand twists all over, letting her hair air dry overnight. The twists were now undone and flowed over her shoulders and down her back. She applied nothing but a little MAC mascara, nude lip liner, and lipstick. She blew herself a kiss in the mirror and was ready to discover what fun lied ahead. Normally the ultimate planner, she decided to wing it on this trip and just enjoy herself. Today, she would explore and do a little sightseeing. She didn't want to think about school, work, O'Shea, Melo, or any other drama for that matter, but no matter what, O'Shea was always in the back of her mind. It was like he was embedded in her heart, and her thoughts would often drift off to the years they spent loving each other. He was even there in her dreams as she slept. She wondered how he was doing and who he was doing. She was just waiting to see what famous chick he would start dating, probably some R&B singer or some shit. You know them ballers love them some R&B divas. That wasn't her business anymore though. She was the one who walked out without a fight, and at this point, she couldn't do a thing but wish him the best despite what happened between them. She recognized the part she played in the failure of their relationship, but he had to be held responsible for his actions too. There was no excuse for what he'd done. He had proven himself disloyal, and that was something she could never get over. As many niggas who came at her, some of which were his own teammates and a few friends, it never crossed her mind to cheat on him.

*Folks stay screaming, 'these hoes ain't loyal', but it's these niggas out here the ones who ain't loyal*, she thought.

She had always done everything O'Shea wanted her to do and more, but the one time she wanted to do her own thing, he wasn't having it. Being cheated on hadn't hurt her confidence any though, which was evident by the way she strutted down the hallway to the elevator on her imaginary runway. She knew her worth, and his actions had nothing to do with something that she lacked. Although she was beautiful, her confidence in herself had nothing to do with looks. It was a confidence and self-worth that had been instilled in her at a very young age. She remembered her father telling her quite often, "Baby girl, not only are you beautiful on the outside, you're even more beautiful on the inside. Kelsey, baby, you are the smartest and funniest girl I know, and you can do anything you set your mind to." He would just repeat the words to her like he was trying to make sure she never forgot them. Even after the crack took him away from her and he turned to the streets, his words stuck with her.

Shaking off the good and bad memories, she decided to focus on the here and now and planned to enjoy herself. As she stood in the elevator, she wore a great big smile. Maybe she would meet a young tender and get her groove back like Stella. Laughing out loud at the thought, she emerged from the elevator catching the attention of most of the men in the lobby, but she ignored their lustful stares as she sashayed to the vehicle waiting outside for her.

*Yeah, this is going to be an interesting trip. I can just feel it*, she thought as her driver pulled off from the curb.

# Chapter Six

*D*ing!
O'Shea heard the sound of the elevator opening as he stood at the desk checking in. The hairs on the back of his neck stood up as he heard a female's laugh and immediately recognized the familiar sound. Her laugh was one that he had heard many times before, one that had been music to his ears for as long as he could remember, but the smile that accompanied that laugh he loved even more.

*It can't be her*, he thought to himself, refusing to turn around and face the truth.

"Damn," he heard the brother in line behind him say while looking in the direction of the woman who had apparently caught the attention of damn near every man in the lobby. O'Shea turned around and only saw the back of her, but he knew at that moment it was Kelsey. The way her ass was bouncing in her dress was all the conformation he needed.

*What the hell is she doing in Jamaica? Is she here with her boyfriend?* The thought of her being there with Romelo had him tight as shit. What were the odds of them being there at the same time, staying at the same resort? *Did she know I was going to be here?* The more O'Shea thought about it, he knew there was no way she would intentionally come knowing that he would be there. When Kelsey walked out of his life two years ago, she made it more than clear that she wanted nothing more to do with him.

"Stay the fuck out of my life and don't ever try to contact me again" was what she told him when he arrived in Dallas trying to convince her to give him another chance. He recalled the pain in her eyes as he pleaded with her through the glass door of her mother's home. He thought she would always be there, but he was wrong and only had himself to blame. He didn't appreciate her, love her, and cherish her like he said he always would.

After signing his big NBA contract, everything changed. He had everyone in his life catering to him, and he wanted Kelsey to fall in line too, but she was too focused on school to worry about him. Due to the lack of attention, he let his ego, the money, and fame come between him and his queen. Kelsey had been his best friend and lover for many years. She was supposed to be his wife one day, but he fucked that up big time. She was smart, beautiful, funny, but most of all, Kelsey was loyal. She gave herself to him when she was just 16, and he was proud to be the first man to make love to her because he never planned on letting her go. That was before he cheated and she walked out of his life…for good. O'Shea never felt more connected to a person than he did to her. They just clicked. He had been with a few other women since she left, but they only made him miss her more. Women gave themselves to him without question. He didn't even have to work for it. He was O'Shea Lewis, an NBA all-star, and for that reason alone, he never knew if women wanted him for him or because he was rich and famous, but he knew for a fact that Kelsey was with him because she really loved him. He came to the realization seven months ago that he missed out on his chance to spend the rest of his life with his one true love. His heart broke all over again the day he found out Kelsey had started seeing someone else.

*** 

*7 Months Earlier…*

Initially, O'Shea told his mother that he wasn't going to be able to make it to the Thanksgiving dinner that was being held at her best friend Anita's home. The pair took turns every year hosting the holiday. He didn't want to run the risk of running into Kelsey, so he came up with an excuse for his mother as to why he wouldn't be attending. He was still too ashamed to face her after what he had done. Vickie was upset at first and hoped that Kelsey wasn't the reason her son wasn't coming home. She always held onto the hope that they would one day get back together. She had never seen two people who loved each more. Later on, Vickie was relieved that O'Shea wouldn't be there after Anita informed her that Kelsey would be attending with a handsome physician named Romelo that she was dating. She didn't want to see her son get his feelings hurt. Kelsey and the doctor seemed to like each other and had been seeing each other for a few months. O'Shea went back and forth with it but decided at the last minute to visit his mother and family for Thanksgiving after all. He realized that he couldn't avoid Kelsey forever. He also hadn't seen his peeps in a minute and was looking forward to hanging out with nothing but family. Being around them always put him in a good mood, and they always treated him the same. He knew that they loved him and had always supported him and his dreams. He decided not to call his mother but would just show up and surprise her for the holiday.

O'Shea arrived at Ms. Anita's right on time. He knew they would be starting dinner at one o'clock sharp like always. He parked his rental and made his way to the house and rang the doorbell. When the door swung open a few seconds later, he almost dropped the cakes he had purchased from a local bakery the day before. His heart was pumping fast as hell and he was at a loss for words. Kelsey always had that effect on him, but she seemed more beautiful than ever. For a while, neither of them moved or said a word. She looked amazing in the sleeveless sweater dress and boots she wore. Kelsey had the ability to make the simplest outfit look sexy as hell. She wore no makeup or jewelry and was still gorgeous to him.

"Hello, Kelsey, it's good to see you," he spoke first.

"Hey, ba…" Before she could finish what she was saying, her date Romelo walked up behind her, wrapping his arms around her waist and kissing her on the cheek.

"Hey, babe, is everything okay?" he asked.

*Babe?* Hearing that term of endearment coming from someone else in reference to his girl was like a slap to the face. Since Kelsey seemed to be at a loss for words too, O'Shea decided to introduce himself after breaking eye contact with her.

"Hey, man, I'm O'Shea, and you are?" He extended his free hand to the man who seemed to be very fond of his Cocoa Baby.

"I know exactly who you are. I'm Romelo. It's nice to meet you, bruh," he said shaking his hand, "Come on, babe, let the man in, so that we can join everyone in the dining room for the prayer."

O'Shea followed the couple to the dining room where the family waited for them. The entire time he felt like ripping the man's hands from around Kelsey's waist and delivering a serious beat down, but he tried to maintain his cool. As soon as he spotted his mother, he put his jealous feelings aside. Vickie immediately started crying as she crossed the room and threw her arms around his neck. He was glad to see her and his other family members. After giving them a moment, his family as well as Kelsey's family gathered around O'Shea, showing him nothing but love.

Dinner was excellent as always. His mother as well as Ms. Anita could throw down in the kitchen. They had taught Kelsey everything she knew, so she was a great cook too. Seeing his family again after months of being away only kept him smiling for so long, and he soon found himself in a foul mood. Seeing Kelsey there with someone else was just too much for him. Watching them interact and smile back and forth had him about to lose it. Dude wasn't just some scrub-ass nigga either. He was a successful black brother, a surgeon. He wasn't corny like O'Shea wished he was because Kelsey couldn't stand a corny-ass nigga. He sat back trying to find something not to like about the dude, but he seemed to have no flaws. The man was perfect, and everyone there seemed to like him too. Even his mom was smitten with Melo, and that pissed O'Shea off even more. He guessed she could sense his bad mood because she grabbed his hand and asked him to help her with something in the kitchen. As soon as they were alone, she went in on him.

"Boy, why the hell you walking around here with your lips poked out?" Vickie asked completely embarrassed by her son's behavior. The least he could do was have some class about himself. She was positive that everyone already knew why he was walking around pouting.

"I don't have my lips poked out. I'm good, Ma…"

"Yeah right, boy. I can see it, so I'm sure that everyone else can see it too. It's written all over your face. Shea, you are here with family. You should try to enjoy yourself. I know it's hard to see Kelsey here with Melo, baby, but I didn't know you would be coming. Had I known, I could've warned you," she told him.

"Oh, so this is not the first time you met him? How long they been seeing each other?" he asked getting all up in his ex's business. It fucked him up to think of Kelsey being with someone else doing all the things that she used to do with him.

"Yes, I've met him once before when she brought him to a party that Anita had. I think they've been together for a few months now," Vickie replied.

"I'm sorry for the attitude, Ma. I'm not going to lie; it's hard as hell being around her right now because I still love that girl. I guess I'll just have to get over it though. If she can do it, so can I," O'Shea said trying to convince himself.

"That's easier said than done, baby. What you shared with Kelsey was special. I don't know what possessed you to do what you did, but we all make mistakes, son. I also have a feeling that she isn't as over you as she appears to be. I suggest you think hard about your next move. You can decide to move on or fight for the one you love. Tell her how much you love and miss her. If anyone can find a way to make things right, I know you can," Vickie said confidently.

"Thanks for the vote of confidence, Ma, but I'll pass. She is definitely over me, but it's all good. It's time for me to go on with my life. I'll always love Cocoa, but I can't go after her because that would be selfish of me. I hurt her, and she deserves to be happy. At this point, I love her enough to let her go. Now, let me get myself together and enjoy this time with the fam. I don't see ya'll enough as it is, so I better take advantage," he said, kissing his mother on her cheek.

Vickie just shook her head. He would find out soon enough that you can't just make love go away, not true love. Shit just didn't work like that. It would make life a lot less complicated if it did, but that just wasn't reality.

"Ok, son, you do what you gotta do, but just remember what your mama told you. I'm sure you'll understand one day."

***

Kelsey was still on edge from her encounter with O'Shea at the door. She almost slipped up and called him "baby". Even years later, it was just still so natural to greet him that way. After all this time, she wasn't even upset like she thought she would be when she saw him. She was actually happy and to say he was looking good would be an understatement. Baby was still fine, and the way he looked at her made her tingle all over. She also noticed the looks he shot Melo throughout the day. She made it a point not to be too affectionate with him in front of O'Shea because she could tell he was feeling some type of way. She knew she shouldn't have cared considering they weren't together anymore, but she couldn't help it. Kelsey decided she needed to get her shit together with the quickness, so she excused herself and went to her old room for a timeout. Everything was just the way it was when she left for college. She studied the picture on her dresser of her brother KJ. He was her everything. His death untimely was tough on everyone, but it hit her especially hard. She also looked at the pictures of her and O'Shea that were all over the place. All the gifts he'd purchased for her over the years were scattered about, and she didn't know why she hadn't already packed all of it away or gotten rid of it. For some reason, she just couldn't bring herself to do it yet. Coming in there didn't seem to be the best decision because all the pictures and memories of them sneaking in there to have sex were clouding her mind only adding fuel to the fire she was feeling down below.

Melo knocked softly on the door and poked his head in interrupting her reminiscing.

"Hey, you okay?"

"I'm good. Come on in," she replied.

"You sure? You've been quiet ever since Mr. Baller showed up," he teased as he took a seat next to her on the bed.

"Whatever," she laughed, "I'm straight." She still felt the same heat between her legs that she'd been feeling since opening the door and seeing O'Shea standing there. She was hot and bothered and decided to use Melo to help her take a little of the edge off.

"I'm just a little tired from work and school is all," Kelsey said using her index finger to trace his jaw line. Finally, she made her way to his lips and he kissed her finger before she replaced it with her lips and began to kiss him. Their kisses started off soft, but before you knew it, they were biting and sucking on each other something serious. In her head, she imagined she was kissing O'Shea.

Melo pushed back. "Hold up, Kelsey, don't start some shit you can't finish. Your mom is liable to come back here looking for you, not to mention all the other people right outside the door. I know we grown and shit, but I'm not trying to have someone bust in and catch us in here fucking," he said breathlessly as she continued to stroke his length through his True Religion jeans. *This girl is a trip*, he thought.

"Hold that thought," she said, hopping up and crossing the room to lock the door. She turned back around, and the look in her eyes told him it was about to be on and popping.

"Fuck it, ain't nothing wrong with a little quickie on Thanksgiving, right?" he said as he pulled out his joint and donned a condom from his wallet. Kelsey left on her thigh high boots and wasted no time lifting up her sweater dress to straddle him and commenced to giving Melo the ride of his life.

\*\*\*

***Twenty Minutes Later…***

O'Shea made a quick run to the restroom before rejoining his family. He was walking with his head down but looked up after bumping into Kelsey as she was coming out of her old bedroom. His hand was now around her waist, and he pulled her into him. The way Kelsey felt, and the way she looked at him, made everything he had just said to his mother go straight out the window. Heat, electricity, and passion flowed between them. Her body seemed to melt into his, and she made no attempt to move away.

He recognized the look in her eyes. He still saw love there. He was almost sure of it until Melo suddenly walked out of her bedroom adjusting his clothing, stopping anything O'Shea wanted to say.

*What the fuck? I know she didn't just fuck this nigga while the whole family was only a few feet away.*

It was just too much for O'Shea to process, so he released her and looked at Melo liked he wanted to beat his ass but just walked away instead. He didn't even bother to look back at Kelsey. It hurt too much.

"What was that all about?" Melo asked.

"Nothing. We just ran into each other," she replied with her heart still pounding.

"Didn't look like nothing to me. What's really going on?" he asked suspiciously.

"Don't start questioning me, Melo. You know what this is between you and me, so let's not get shit twisted," Kelsey said becoming irritated. Melo wasn't her man, and she had to remind him of that before he got beside himself.

"Chill out with all that attitude. All I'm saying is I know that you were in a relationship with him for a long time. Maybe you still have feelings for him or something. It would definitely explain why you don't want to take our relationship to the next level. I know things started out as just casual, but I want more now, and you just refuse to let me in. We get along great, and I really enjoy your company. You enjoy being with me too, don't you, Kelsey?" he asked sounding desperate.

"Damn, Melo, why are you tripping? I've been over Shea for a long time now, so he has nothing to do with what's going on between us. And of course I enjoy kicking it with you, but I like things the way they are. I'm not looking for anything serious, and if you can't get with that then maybe we need to chill for a while cause I don't want to keep having this conversation with you."

She had no reason to be this rude to Melo and actually she was more upset at herself than she was with him. After all this time, O'Shea still made her feel like a silly-ass love-sick school girl. He was the reason she and Melo were fucking around in her bedroom in the first place because he had her hormones all over the place. It had been so long since she had been in his presence, and it had her slightly off her game.

"You're right. Maybe we do need to chill for a minute," Melo said before going to say goodbye to her mother and other family members. He was hoping that she would eventually change her mind and see that they were good together. She was right about him knowing what was up from the beginning, but he didn't think he would get so into her. She was different from any other woman he had ever dated. She was amazing in every way, and he wanted her all for himself.

Kelsey got herself together and made sure to only come out after she knew Romelo was gone. She wasn't about to kiss his ass because that wasn't her style. She didn't stay long after his departure. She collected the leftovers her mother packed up as well as the chess pie that Vickie made just for her before saying her goodbyes.

\*\*\*

O'Shea had gone outside with Kelsey's cousin Nate to see his restored 1970 Chevy SS. He had done a lot of work to the car since the last time he'd seen it, and it was definitely a beauty. Nate was a dope boy back in the day, but from the looks of things, he had toned it down in the last few years. You could tell he was all about his family these days. His daughter Kennedi was the cutest little girl, and she had her daddy wrapped around her tiny finger. O'Shea wanted kids too, but Kelsey was the only woman he wanted to bear his children, so the subject was on the back burner indefinitely.

"So, O'Shea, man, what's been up?" Nate asked as they posted up at the back of the car drinking Coronas.

"Just ball, man. I don't really have time for nothing else."

"This shit is weird, bro," he said as he shook his head.

"What's that?"

"You being here and Kelsey being with somebody else. Don't get me wrong, dude is cool and all, but it's just weird that you two aren't together anymore, man. I mean since we was kids that's all I've known is 'Shea and Kelsey'. When I saw her, I saw you. You mufuckas was on some soul mate shit for real," he laughed.

"The shit is crazy to me too, but, hey, I messed up, so it is what it is. Moms had to pull me to the side and check me about how I was acting. Seeing her with that nigga had me heated, and I didn't even realize it. I can't be mad at her for moving on, but I ain't gone lie, it got me kind of fucked up in the head, you know what I mean?"

"Yeah, I know, big dawg, but for real though, I know my cousin, man, and I really think she still got feelings for you," Nate told him.

"You think so?" O'Shea asked. He thought he saw something there too when he ran into in the hallway, but he could have been mistaken.

"Yeah, man, I think she's just hanging with 'ol boy to pass the time. He is way more into her than she is into him. I pay attention to shit like that. I saw how you two were with one another, and this thing she got going with him is definitely not the same. I think you still have a chance to make it work with her."

"Honestly, Nate, I don't even think I deserve another chance, man. I fucked up so bad last time she probably won't ever forgive me."

"Fuck what you talking about, fam. Everyone deserves a second chance. I won't lie and say it's going to be easy because I saw firsthand how hurt Kelsey was when you hooked up with that reality-star bitch, but look at my situation with Michelle. Shit, I used to fuck around on her all the damn time, and she finally got tired and left my black-ass. I thought I was gone die without my girl, man. She stayed away for almost a year, and her being gone let me know I wasn't shit without her. I was literally sick. I couldn't eat, couldn't sleep, nothing. Chelle had held me down all those years, and I didn't do right by her. When she decided to give me one last chance, I knew there wasn't a person on this earth who could get me to step out on my lady again. Man, I ain't even giving these hoes a second look out here in these streets. We've been going strong ever since, and when God blessed us with Kennedi, I knew I would never let anything tear us apart again. If Chelle could find it in her heart to forgive me after all my bullshit, I'm sure Kels can forgive you for one fuck up."

"Man, I hope you're right, and I'm glad you and Chelle were able to work things out. Hopefully, Kelsey and I will find our way back to each other because I know for a fact that I will never find what we had with the next bitch. These hoes out here thirsty as hell for fame, and I'm not about to let no bitch come up off of me, so I be curving they fake asses left and right. My niggas be tripping out on me because I be turning down so much pussy," O'Shea said as they both laughed, "Then you got people on your team trying to set you up with actresses, models, and singers. I ain't trying to fuck with nobody on no publicity shit, man. Kelsey was the only one 'with me shooting in the gym', and that was way before we even started fucking around. Cocoa's as trill as they come, and I miss her black-ass."

"Don't feel bad, fam. I bet she miss yo' ass too. My cousin is just too stubborn to admit it."

They continued to chop it up until Kelsey walked outside causing O'Shea to pause mid-sentence.

"You gone, kinfolk?" Nate asked.

"Yeah, cuz, I'm on-call tomorrow, so I gotta go home and get some rest." She avoided making eye contact with Shea but could feel his eyes on her.

"A'ight, I'll see you next weekend for Kennedi's birthday party. You still coming through, right?"

"Hell yeah, you know my god baby ain't gone let me miss her party. She called me the other day to let me know what she wanted, so I went shopping yesterday to pick up everything she asked for plus some things I wanted her to have," Kelsey replied smiling. She was actually looking forward to celebrating with her little cousin that next weekend.

"You need to quit spoiling my baby yo'," he laughed.

"You know that's my girl, so I gotta hook her up. Besides, I'm never having kids, so I might as well spend all this money on my boo. I'll see you Saturday, cousin." She turned to leave, but before she opened the door to her Audi coupe, she looked back and made eye contact with O'Shea again. "It was good seeing you, Shea. Have a safe trip home," she smiled.

He smiled back before he said, "Thank you, Cocoa Baby. Take care of yourself."

He was hoping her choice to not have children had nothing to do with him, but deep down inside, he was sure it did. That made him feel like shit because Kelsey always talked about them having at least ten kids. He told her they could have three at the most, but he knew he would give her as many as she wanted because he loved her that much. Kelsey shook her head and was smiling even harder now, remembering the nickname he'd given her when they were younger.

"You do the same," she said before she hopped in her ride and dipped to her place in Uptown Dallas.

When she made it home, she got a call from Melo apologizing for his behavior at dinner. He admitted that he agreed to a sex-only relationship and had no right to try to change up on her. He told her he wanted to still to see her and they could continue on as they were before. Kelsey was glad to hear it because she didn't want to get rid of him just yet. She had a strong sexual appetite and didn't want to lose her cuddy buddy. She had fucked around with two other dudes prior to hooking up with Melo, but he was the only one who held her attention past a few months. She knew it would be hard to find someone she could actually have an intelligent conversation with and also assist her in fucking up a few headboards from time to time. If she were in a different place, she could see herself with Melo for the long haul, but there was something about him that held her back. She couldn't put her finger on it, so they would remain in this space until he decided he no longer wanted to do things her way. At that point, Kelsey would just move on. She apologized to him for being so rude and asked if he wanted to come over and finish what they started in her bedroom at her mother's house. Of course, he happily agreed.

# Chapter Seven

After laying on the bed rehashing the past, O'Shea decided to stay in his suite for the remainder of the day. He wasn't ready to run into Kelsey just yet. He picked up the phone to call and check on his mother instead.

"Hello," she sang into the receiver.

"Hey, Ma," he said happy to hear her voice.

"Hey, son, how are you, baby?" Vickie asked just as excited to hear from him.

"I'm great, Ma. How you doing? How was your doctor's appointment on Friday?"

He worried about his mother often after her cancer scare two years ago, but she seemed to be doing a lot better now. He knew he needed to spend more time with her and planned to visit for a few weeks after he returned to the states.

"Everything went good, baby. When you coming to Dallas to see me?" she asked not wanting to discuss her follow-up.

"I'll be there soon. Right now I'm on vacation in Jamaica."

"Jamaica?" She was hoping that he and Kelsey were there together. Anita told her that Kelsey would be in Jamaica for a week as well. She prayed that they had come to their senses and got back together. When she first found out the reason behind their breakup, she was very upset with her son. She knew O'Shea loved him some Kelsey and felt that he had made a big mistake when he cheated on her. She just hoped her son smartened up and went after what he wanted before it was too late. Kelsey's friend Romelo was quite the charmer, but Vickie knew that she still loved O'Shea and would definitely be her daughter-in-law one day. She prayed that it would happen before her time came to go on to glory. "How long will you be there?"

"It was just a last minute trip, but I'll be here for about a week. I just decided I needed some time away from the real world," he told her. It was off season, and without a significant other in his life, he had a lot of free time on his hands. During the season, he had basketball to focus on, but without Kelsey in his life, living his dreams didn't mean as much. He missed her terribly, and he hoped that her being there too was a sign from God. O'Shea thought of her constantly and hoped one day they could move past his mistake and give their relationship another try. They really needed to talk, but he was unsure if Kelsey was ready to hear him out.

"Did you go alone?" she asked sounding hopeful.

"Yes, ma'am. Why do you ask?"

"No reason, just curious is all."

"Ok, well, I'm glad everything went okay at your follow-up. I just wanted to call to check in and let you know how much I love you, Ma."

"I love you too, son. Enjoy your trip and thank you again for my new car. I thought it was a bit too much at first, but I have to admit I really do love it, Shea."

"No problem, and nothing will ever be too much for you. You've sacrificed so much in your life for me, and I just wanted to show my appreciation."

Although he wasn't her biological son, Vickie had loved him and cared for O'Shea his entire life.

He was grateful that she was the person his birth mother chose to raise him. His real mother was raped at 17-years old and ended up getting pregnant by her attacker. Unable to cope with what had happened to her, she took her own life just weeks after giving birth to him. O'Shea was already living with Vickie, so she went through the process and adopted him. Before he came into her life, she had been married, but her husband ended up leaving her for his secretary when they found out she couldn't have children of her own, and they had two kids together. The cold thing about that was his new wife ended up abandoning her family for another man, leaving him stuck with the children. He even tried to come back to Vickie so they could have a mother, but she wasn't having it. That bitch named Karma is not to be fucked with. Vickie loved children though and longed to be a mother someday herself, but it just wasn't in the cards for her. That's probably the reason she was always caring for other folk's kids. When God saw fit to bless her with O'Shea, she couldn't have been happier. She loved him like she had given birth to him herself.

"I know, baby, and I love you."

Tears clouded her eyes, and she hoped her son couldn't hear it in her voice. Her follow-up hadn't gone as well as she let on. Her Oncologist informed her some months back that her cancer had returned and spread to other areas of her body. At that time, he only gave her a few more months at the most, and her appointment on Friday only reinforced what she had already been told at her previous visit. She declined to do another round of chemotherapy and radiation months ago. Her body was just tired, and she wanted to enjoy the rest of the time she had with her loved ones. O'Shea would be visiting in two weeks, and she would discuss her prognosis with him then. She needed time to let it all sink in, but most of all, she wanted him to enjoy his trip. Anita was devastated and tried to convince her to try one more round of chemo, but she refused. Anita knew just as well as she did that it wouldn't do much good seeing as how the cancer had spread, but she didn't want to lose her best friend. The two had been friends for many years and worked at the same hospital on the same unit until Vickie's health required her to retire early.

O'Shea talked to his mom for a few more minutes before ending the call. He was looking forward to seeing her when he got back home. Hearing her voice put him in a better mood, so he changed his mind about not leaving the suite.

***

It was nearing sunset as Kelsey strolled along the beach. She had enjoyed her day and was finally feeling at peace. It had been so long since she had some real chill time. School and work had been her life for the last year and a half. After taking six months off after her breakup with O'Shea, she went back completely focused, and it paid off. She finally achieved her dream of becoming a Nurse Practitioner and had accepted a position in the Gastroenterology Department where she currently worked. She was looking forward to starting her job and beginning a new chapter in her life.

Exhausted, she decided to go back to her room and relax a little. She was carrying her sandals in one hand and a large beach bag in the other when suddenly she noticed this fine-ass brother stretched out on a lounge chair not far from where she stood. He had on shades and looked to be sleeping by the rise and fall of his chest.

*Damn*, she thought as she admired his beautifully sculpted body. The tattoos that covered his arms, neck, and chest really set it off for her.

Suddenly, she noticed something familiar about the man that stopped her dead in her tracks. *The fuck?* She recognized the big-ass 'KELSEY' tattoo across his chest. She and O'Shea got each other's names tatted while attending college at Baylor. His name ran vertical down her right side. He had added some ink since then, but she recognized her name immediately. Her heart rate increased, and she felt scorching hot all over despite the nice cool breeze coming through. Her feet seemed to move on their own and didn't stop until she stood directly in front of him, gawking at his sexy-ass as he slept.

O'Shea had fallen asleep but was jolted out of his nap by a familiar feeling. When he opened his eyes, he couldn't believe the beauty that was standing in front of him. At first, he thought he was dreaming but soon realized that she was really there. Kelsey looked gorgeous. He had to remove his shades to get a better view of her.

"The fuck you doing in Jamaica, O'Shea?" she asked with her hand on her hip looking too good.

"Woman, I see you still curse like a sailor," he laughed as he stretched out his arms and sat up.

His comment made her laugh as well. He used to get on her case all the time about her foul mouth, and she hated it. Now she could only laugh because that was one thing he couldn't change about her.

"Hell yeah, you know that ain't ever gon' change."

"The question I have is what are you doing here?" he replied while blatantly checking her out from head to toe. He definitely liked what he saw. The two piece bathing suit she was wearing left little to the imagination, and her body was pure perfection. His Cocoa Baby was still killing shit.

"I graduated a few weeks ago and decided to treat myself to a vacation before I start my new gig. I've been here since Monday and plan to fly back to Dallas on Monday. How about you? How long you here for?" After she didn't receive a response, she spoke again. "O'Shea, did you hear me?"

"My bad. What did you say?" he asked snapping back to reality. He was so busy checking her out that he hadn't heard a thing she said.

"I said I'm treating myself to a vacation to celebrate graduation, and I asked how long you'll be here?" she replied smiling. She didn't miss him checking her out and was flattered that he still couldn't keep his eyes off of her.

"So you finally made your dream come true, huh? Congratulations, Kelsey. I'm really happy for you."

"Thanks, Shea. So how long will you be here?" she asked for the third time.

"I fly out on Tuesday, and then I'll be in Dallas a week after that to see my mom."

"I cannot fucking believe that we came here at the same time," she said shaking her head.

"We always planned to come to Jamaica, and since I had some free time, I decided to make it happen. You know, do some things I've always wanted to do and visit all the places that we used to talk about."

"I know right," Kelsey said suspiciously. She wondered if he'd known that she would be there. She hoped that this wasn't some set up planned by their mothers. She had a feeling Anita wouldn't do that knowing how she felt about O'Shea, so she tossed the idea out right away. She also wondered if he was in Jamaica alone because the last thing she needed was to be there in this magnificent place alone only to see him flossing around with some bitch in her face. She still had feelings for him, and honestly, she couldn't handle seeing him with someone else.

"Have a seat. Let's catch up," he said breaking her out of her short daydream, "So did you come here alone, or did you bring 'Dr. Feel-good' with you?"

"For your information, Melo is not here. I came alone, and why the hell he gotta be 'Dr. Feel-good'?" she asked as she took the seat next to him.

"Oh, you know why," he said referring to their run-in at Thanksgiving. Just thinking about her fucking that nigga still made his chest hurt, so he hurried to change the subject. He hated that he had even brought it up. "I'm here solo too, just wanted to get away for a minute."

"Yeah, so did I," she replied as she blushed remembering the holiday. She was blushing because he was the real reason she had messed around with Melo in her room that day. Seeing him standing there in the doorway looking so handsome had her wet and ready just like she was when she spotted him a moment ago.

As they sat together, she felt so at ease talking with him. It was just like old times, and it was too much. O'Shea had her going in circles. One minute, she was chill, but when she felt herself getting too relaxed, she started to freak out a little. She wanted to keep up the brick wall she had built intact. To make that happen, she needed to keep her distance, so Kelsey rose from her chair to put some space between them.

"I'm about to head back to my room and lay down for a while. I've been out and about all day, and I'm completely pooped. I guess I'll see you later, Shea," Kelsey said attempting to walk away.

"Give me a second. I'm about to head in too, so I'll just walk with you," he said as he put on his shirt and gathered his belongings.

While he did that, she used the time to put her sandals back on. From the corner of her eye, she noticed him peeping at her ass as she bent over. *Same old Shea*, she thought, *Always was a sucker for the booty*.

"Mama is going to trip out when I tell her that I ran into you here," she said once they started walking.

"Well, I talked to Ma this morning, and she already knows I'm here, so with that being said, I'm sure Anita already has been informed by now. Give me your bag." She handed her bag to him without hesitation, and when their hands touched, a familiar heat passed between them. Kelsey was sure he felt it too, but neither of them said anything and continued to walk. It was crazy that they still got this way around each other despite how much time had passed.

Neither of them spoke a word on the way back as they were both consumed with thoughts of one another. When they arrived at the hotel entrance, Kelsey attempted to take her bag from O'Shea and tell him goodbye, but he continued walking through the door.

"You're staying here too?" she asked surprised.

"I am. At least for the next seven days. Crazy, right? We always talked about coming here, and without even knowing it, we ended up here at the same time, staying at the same place. When I saw you, I couldn't believe it."

Kelsey had no idea that he saw her in the hotel lobby earlier. "Likewise," she replied feeling a tad uneasy. How was she going to enjoy her time there knowing he was so close by? "It was good seeing you, but like I said I'm kind of tired, so a shower and nap are on my to-do list."

"I feel you." He was about to say goodbye and go on about his business when he remembered the party that some of the other tourists mentioned to him earlier. "Hey, I heard about a cool little party tonight that's supposed to be pretty hype. If you're not too tired later, you should come through. Could be a lot of fun," O'Shea said handing her the folded up flyer from his pocket.

"Like I said I'm pretty exhausted, but if I decide to go, I'll see you there I guess."

She turned to walk toward the elevator, and there it was—the plump luscious-ass he had fallen in love with all those years before. He had caressed, squeezed, and licked every part of that thang. His mouth began to water, and a shiver passed through his body just thinking about the things they used to do in bed together. Her bikini was solid white, and the bottoms were barely big enough to contain all that ass. The color against her chocolate skin was a sight to see, and Kelsey had no shame in her game. She wore no cover up, just a two piece and some designer gladiator sandals. Her confidence was one of the things he admired most about her. Cocoa was bad in every way, and she knew it. He missed making love to her, but most of all, he missed their friendship. They'd shared so much and had been the best of friends for many years. He wanted that back more than anything.

"A'ight, hopefully, I'll see you later."

# Chapter Eight

Kelsey didn't plan on showing up to the party but later decided that there was no reason for her to dodge O'Shea. Before they started dating, they were friends first, so it seemed silly to stay cooped up in her room because of the way she felt when she was around him. It was obvious that they still shared a strong attraction to one another, but that was no reason to not enjoy her time in Jamaica. After a two hour nap, she showered, got dressed, and was on her way out of the door. She came there to have a good time, and that's exactly what she planned to do.

O'Shea wasn't there once she arrived, so she went over to the bar and ordered herself a rum with pineapple juice when she noticed an attractive guy eyeing her at the other end of the bar. She smiled letting him know it was okay to approach her, and on cue, he excused himself from his boys and walked over. They made small talk, and she learned his name was Terrence. He was from Brooklyn and was in Jamaica on vacation with his line brothers. He was a caramel cutie, and she loved the neat locs that fell down to his shoulders. He asked her if she was there alone, and Kelsey lied telling him that she was there with a friend, but her friend decided to stay in. She didn't know him well enough and didn't want him all up in her business. She figured if Shea decided not to come, at least she could pass the time and enjoy the company of another handsome man. Terrence asked

Kelsey to dance, and she agreed. They made their way to the dance floor already bobbing and swaying because the DJ was on fire and the party was getting live.

Kelsey knew the exact moment that O'Shea walked into the party. She could feel him watching her and didn't have to look his way to know exactly where he was standing. She tried her best to ignore him and keep her eyes closed as she grooved to the reggae music that played. When she finally looked O'Shea's way, she wished she hadn't because she couldn't hide the lust in her eyes even if she tried. He looked good enough to eat, and just like many other occasions, she began to heat up. He was dressed in all black—a black Tom Ford t-shirt with the number '61' on the sleeves, black Tom Ford jeans, and black Buscemi high-top leather sneakers. He was fine as fuck, and Kelsey wasn't the only one who noticed. Other women were checking him out too, but he wasn't paying attention because his eyes were glued to hers. Her dance partner was good looking too and was putting down his game down proper, but Terrence didn't have anything on O'Shea.

*Fuck what I said earlier. I don't know how I'm going to be in the same vicinity as this man for the next five days and keep my composure, let alone my legs closed,* Kelsey thought to herself.

*** 

At first, O'Shea didn't think Kelsey was going to show up, but once he spotted her, he watched her closely as she danced with some buff-ass nigga with dreads. She looked good in her teal green romper and gold accessories. The outfit fit her just right and hugged her round-ass perfectly. The gold strappy heels she wore made her legs look long and luscious. She hadn't noticed him yet, so O'Shea decided to stand back and watch her dance. Her hips moved seductively as she swayed with her eyes closed. When she finally opened them and looked his way, O'Shea could tell she liked what she saw by the way she licked her top lip. That had always been her signal that she wanted him, and he received the message loud and clear. The guy she was dancing with bent down to whisper something to her that had her smiling. At that moment, O'Shea decided it was time to go over and cut in. Whatever 'ol boy thought was popping off tonight, he was sadly mistaken because O'Shea wasn't having that shit. Kelsey wasn't his woman anymore, but she wasn't dread head's either.

Kelsey and O'Shea never took their eyes off one another as he walked over to her. She immediately recognized the look in O'Shea's eyes and knew she was going to have to get rid of her new found friend before he did it for her.

"Hey, Cocoa, may I have this dance?" O'Shea asked standing to the side of her. He didn't even bother acknowledging Terrence, who looked a bit confused but concluded that this must have been the 'friend' she mentioned earlier. He could tell they knew one another by the way they looked at each other, like he wasn't even standing there. The plan was to have her back in his suite fucking her brains out by the end of the night, but it didn't look like that would be happening after all.

"Sure," she said still looking at O'Shea, "Thanks for the dance, Terrence." He nodded and walked away with his head held high. The room was full of available women, and he knew he wouldn't be sleeping alone.

A slow jam started right on time, and they began to move. With his hand around her waist, O'Shea pulled her close to him. He inhaled lightly when he felt her hard nipples graze his chest.

*Damn, she smells good*, he thought as she laid her head on his chest. After dancing for a while, Kelsey tilted her head up to look at him. He stared back down at her, and it seemed as though he was looking through to her soul. If that was actually possible, he would be able to see that she still loved him very much. She never stopped, but even though she had forgiven him for hurting her, she doubted that she would ever forget it.

"What you thinking about?" he wanted to know.

"Thinking about how much fun we used to have. It seems like it was so long ago." Kelsey really wanted to tell him that she missed him but she couldn't.

"It wasn't that long ago, and we did have some great times. The best times of my life," O'Shea said still looking her directly in her eyes. He wanted her to feel everything he was about to say. "I'm so sorry that I hurt you, Kelsey. I don't ever think I'll forgive myself for doing that to you. That one mistake cost me what meant everything to me," he said sincerely.

"It is what it is, Shea. We can't change the past. If we could, I would change some of the things I've done too, but I can't and neither can you. Life doesn't always turn out the way we want it to, but it does go on, you know? You should forgive yourself because I've forgiven you."

"You have?" he asked surprised.

"Of course, I have. I realize that you didn't set out to hurt me. You just got caught up. I mean, I know that you loved me and I loved you, but sometimes love just isn't enough, you know what I mean?"

*Did she just say 'loved' as in past tense?*

The fact that she hinted at no longer loving him hurt deeply because he was still very much in love with her. "Yeah I know what you mean. I'm glad that you're here, and we had the opportunity to talk like this." He escorted her to an available table and got them both a drink. Hell, he needed a strong one after this conversation, but it was long overdue. "So, how are things with you and the doctor?" O'Shea asked changing the subject.

"Melo and I are fine I guess. He understands that I don't want a serious relationship. I've been too focused on school and work. I'm just trying to kick it right now."

"And he's cool with that?"

"Well, he was for the first few months, but now he's trying to change the game. He wants more than I'm willing to give." She paused for a moment and then went on to say, "Let me be honest with you, Shea. I just want someone to have some bomb-ass sex with and take me on a date every now and then. If he can't get with that then I'm gon' have to cut his ass loose. I even told him he's free to see other people."

"Really?" The Kelsey he remembered would've never be into that type of relationship. Not being with him seemed to bring out her independent and rebellious side. O'Shea had to admit that he liked it, but she could have kept the part about sexing the good doctor to herself. He was trying to be her friend, but he wasn't ready to hear all that.

"Well, yeah, I don't want him to miss out on meeting someone special waiting on me to come around. I mean, he really is a great guy, and he deserves someone he can build with. I'm just not the one though."

"Is it okay for you to see other people too?" he asked as an idea popped in his head.

"If I wanted to, yes, but I'm not really cool with dealing with more than one person at a time. It's not my style," she said hoping he didn't think she was trying to be funny, "Why do you ask?"

"I'm asking because…"

"Because?" Kelsey asked with her hand up waiting for his response.

"Would you ever consider seeing me?" He decided to go on and throw it out there.

She was shocked by his question and couldn't answer him right away. She just sat there stunned, looking at him like he was fucking crazy.

"Look, Kelsey, we already know each other, and I'm not looking to get serious with anyone right now either," he continued, knowing it was a straight up lie. If she was down, he would use it as an opportunity to win her back.

"I can't believe you would even ask me something like that, O'Shea. Don't you think that would be too weird considering our history? It's just too much," she said shaking her head in disbelief.

"I guess it could be kind of weird or it could be exciting. A little fun in the sun and a lot of sex on the beach while we're here in Jamaica," he replied mischievously.

"I don't think so, Shea. Let's just talk about something else because you've obviously lost your mind," Kelsey said sipping her drink nervously.

"Just hear me out…," he started, but she cut him off.

"Shea, just stop. I don't want to talk about this, okay? I really can't believe you right now."

After everything that had happened, he had the nerve to think she would be cool with something like that. She was pissed, but she was even more upset with herself because she actually wanted to say yes.

"I'm going to head back to my room because you're tripping," she said getting up from the table. She couldn't agree to his proposition because she knew that it would only cause her more heartache in the long run. When she was almost to the exit, O'Shea caught up to her and gently placed his hand on her arm.

"Look, Kelsey, I'm sorry that I even suggested what I did back there," he said regretfully. The conversation was going great and he just had to fuck it up. He saw an opportunity and jumped on it without thinking of her feelings, and he felt terrible. "I understand what you're saying. We do have history, and it probably wouldn't be a good idea for us to engage in that type of relationship. I apologize because you mean way more to me than just having someone to share a bed with on vacation."

"Thanks, Shea. Apology accepted," she said loosening up a bit.

"But let me ask you just one question..."

"What is it, Shea?" she asked rolling her eyes. She was thinking that he was about to start up with the same mess again.

"You've forgiven me for what happened between us, and you've moved on, right?"

"Yes, I have," she answered.

"Ok then, were both here in Jamaica at the same time. Let's just enjoy it together like two old friends.

Let's sight see and do all the other shit we said we would if we ever came here. The only difference is we aren't together anymore. How does that sound?"

"I don't know, Shea. Give me tonight to think about it, and I'll let you know, okay?"

"Bet. Can we meet for breakfast in the morning? You can let me know then and just so you know, I promise to be on my very best behavior," he said with his right hand up.

"That's cool. I'll see you in the morning, Shea."

"Tomorrow morning," he nodded.

He watched her walk away, her hips swaying sexily from side to side. The romper she wore crisscrossed on her back and her ass looked plump and juicy. It seemed as though she was putting a little extra sway in her hips, but it could have just been his imagination.

*** 

*Why the fuck did I put on that little show for O'Shea when I was walking off?* Kelsey asked herself, *I tell the man I don't want hook up with him for old-time sake then I turn around and do the sexy walk for him.*

He used to love to see her do her sexy big booty walk. She knew his ass was watching too. Kelsey smiled as she looked back only to catch him standing there with that look in his eyes, a look she knew all too well.

In the shower, Kelsey thought about O'Shea's proposition. *It could be a lot of fun to hang out with him.* The problem was she couldn't be around him and not crave his touch, his tongue, or his ten-inch caramel magic stick. Chills passed through her body just thinking about that part of him as the hot water sprayed down on her naked body. When she was in his presence, all of those familiar feelings would resurface, and she didn't think she could handle it. After a few more minutes of going back and forth with herself, she decided to give in to temptation and accept O'Shea's proposal with a few added benefits. As good as Romelo was in bed, he didn't come close to O'Shea. The love and the connection she shared with him made the sex ten times better. She would agree to spend the next five days with him, but she wanted the experience that they had always planned, including the sex on the beach. They could explore Jamaica during the day and spend their nights together in bed. Five days filled with being tourists, having sex, and partying sounded like a plan to her. At the end of their trip, they would go their separate ways full of memories of what occurred between them in paradise. Kelsey knew she was playing with fire because she still had feelings for him but knew it didn't matter. She had to have him.

Since making the decision to hook up with O'Shea, she had been on fire. Kelsey wanted him bad, and she tossed and turned all night unable to sleep. The sex toy she brought with her didn't even come close to giving her any relief, and it usually did the job. She knew O'Shea was the only one who could quench the inferno that was burning inside of her, but she wondered if he would go for her new proposition. There was only one way to find out.

*Ask and you shall receive.*

# Chapter Nine

O'Shea was sitting at a table in the dining area the following morning waiting for Kelsey to arrive when he noticed a group of women, one in particular, kept sizing him up with her eyes. He looked away without smiling, hoping she would take the hint. She was cute enough, but his mind was elsewhere. His thoughts were on Kelsey and if she would accept his offer. He wanted her back, but at this point, if friendship was all she wanted, he would take what he could get.

"In deep thought, huh?" O'Shea looked up and saw it was the chick from the table across from him. Alex recognized him from seeing him play basketball for LA. When she first spotted him, she couldn't help but think that today was her lucky day. She was also in Jamaica from LA and was vacationing with friends. She had dated one of his teammates and met O'Shea at a party thrown at her then boyfriend's house. O'Shea had a girlfriend at the time too, but word on the street was they had broken up a while back. Although she had been in his presence before, Alex was sure that he didn't remember her and for that she was glad.

"Yes, I guess you could say that," he replied dryly.

"Do you want some company?"

"No, thanks," he said sitting straight up. She looked surprised that he turned down her offer to join him. Obviously, she couldn't tell that he didn't really feel like being bothered.

"Are you sure?" she asked, placing her hand on her hip purposely moving her cover up to the side and giving him a close up of her tiny waist, wide hips, and sexy bikini.

"Actually, I'm waiting on my girl to join me," he lied hoping to scare her off. She was attractive, but he was turned off by her aggressive approach. Plus, he didn't want Kelsey to walk up and think he was trying to holla at this bitch, so she needed to get lost quick.

"You sure I can't keep you company until she gets here?" Alex asked boldly, stepping closer to him. O'Shea guessed she thought he would be moved by the skimpy bikini she wore along with her enhanced ass and breasts, but she was wrong. He liked the real thing, and the girl he wanted was as real as they came. Females these days had no chill. He tried to turn her down nicely, but her dehydrated ass just didn't get it. He was about to give her the real, but before he could respond, he noticed Kelsey walking up behind the chick.

"Naw, lil' mama, I'm all the company he needs," Kelsey said with an amused look on her face.

She was dressed down but still cute, wearing some short khaki shorts with a white wife beater and a pair of red monochrome Chucks. She wore her hair down, and it was beautiful with loose curls flowing wildly around her chocolate face. O'Shea assumed she heard some of their conversation and hoped she was willing to play the role of his 'girlfriend' at least for a moment.

"Hey, love, I've been waiting on you." He got up from the table kissing her cheek.

"Sorry to have bothered you. You two enjoy your breakfast," Alex said as she walked off embarrassed by her failed attempt to snag another baller.

"I was beginning to think you weren't coming," he said as he held out her chair for her to sit down before joining her at the table.

"Sorry, I'm late, but I over slept. I had a hard time falling asleep last night."

"Looks like we both had the same problem."

"Oh, really? And what were you thinking about that kept you up?"

"I was thinking of what your answer would be to the suggestion I made last night."

Kelsey took a moment to think about what she was about to do. She was taking a big risk with her heart, but it was what she wanted. She didn't want to catch feelings again, just have a little fun.

*Fuck it, here goes nothing.* "My answer is yes, but I want the full experience, Shea."

When she licked her top lip, he already knew what was up. "What do you mean by that, Cocoa?" he asked not wanting to assume anything.

"What I mean is I want to experience everything we planned if we came here together. I want it all…including you, at least for the next five days anyway. At the end of our trip, you go your way and I'll go mines."

"Let me get this straight. You want to take me up on my original offer, but then we're supposed to just act as if nothing happened once we get back home?" He couldn't believe what he was hearing, but he was with it.

"That's exactly what I'm saying," she confirmed.

"You think you can handle that?" he challenged. Her attitude sure had changed drastically from the night before, but he wasn't complaining.

"I know I can. The question is can you handle it?"

This is a dangerous game we're playing if we go through with it. Honestly, I might not want to give it back if you give it to me again, Cocoa," he said with a devilish grin, "I might enjoy it too much and want to make it mines again." His dick was already jumping just thinking about making love to her pretty-ass.

"Oh, I know you'll enjoy it, but you won't have a choice but to give it back, O'Shea. Do you need some time to think about it? If so, let me know soon because I'll only be here for five more days," she added as if it didn't matter to her either way.

"No, no, baby girl, I don't need more time. I'm down for whatever, so….what do we do first?"

"Each other," she stated boldly shrugging her shoulders

"You sure you don't want to have breakfast first?" he asked laughing.

With a mischievous grin spread across her face, she stated, "No baby, I'm hungry for something else right now."

*Damn, I love this girl*, he thought to himself. "Lead the way then, Cocoa Baby!"

***

As soon as they entered the suite, they went at it—kissing, touching, and rubbing as all those familiar feelings resurfaced for them both. The sparks were definitely flying. O'Shea wanted to slow things down and savor the moment, but he was having a difficult time getting himself under control.

His dick was rock solid, and he craved her in the worst way. Thank goodness they needed to breathe and had no other choice but to break off the kiss. The look Kelsey gave him let him know that she was just as on fire as he was, so he placed his hands on both sides of her beautiful face as they looked into one another's eyes before he lowered his mouth to hers again. He kissed her slowly and sensually causing her to moan. O'Shea broke off the kiss again only to pull her tank over her head and noticed she wasn't wearing a bra underneath. She was so sexy to him, and he missed making love to her and planned on taking full advantage of the time they had together. It was then that he realized that he hadn't come prepared, and she noticed the frustrated look on his face.

"What's wrong?" she moaned as she traced her tongue along his jawline.

"I didn't bring any condoms," he replied with disappointment.

"No worries," she said, walking over to the table located on the side of the bed. Kelsey opened the drawer and pulled out a pack of Magnums and held them up. She tossed the box his way and proceeded to remove her shoes and bottoms. "Now that we got that out of the way, you want to hurry up and get out of those clothes? I need you inside me like yesterday," she said with a hint of desperation in her voice.

"Come over here and undress me then, Kelsey," he ordered.

She did as she was told and crossed the room to join him. She removed his clothing all the way down to his Polo boxer briefs. She then stood on her tip toes, wrapped her arms around his neck, and offered him her luscious lips. O'Shea took them without hesitation as he picked her up and moved toward the bed. He sat her down, and she rose up on her knees continuing to kiss him passionately. He turned her around and began massaging her breasts and placing kisses on the nape of her neck. His hands made their way down and gently squeezed her pussy. He found that she was soaking wet as he used his index finger and thumb to massage her clit. When he knew she was on the verge of an orgasm, he pushed her down and began eating her pussy from the back. He had her ass tooted up in the air as he licked, nibbled, and sucked on her peach. She was even sweeter than he remembered. Kelsey was going wild, moaning and grabbing at the covers that sat crumpled off to the side. She screamed out as she came back to back causing a waterfall to drip down the inside of her thighs turning him on even more. He loved how gushy she got during sex.

*What in the entire fuck?* Kelsey thought.

She had never had her pussy eaten like that before. She laid there for a few seconds before she looked back to find him wearing a satisfied grin on his face. He knew he had done his thing, but she was prepared though.

*I got something for his ass*, she said to herself, just as eager to please him. After instructing him to lay down and placing a satin scarf over his eyes, she walked over to the table and retrieved the grapefruit she had placed in warm water earlier. She prepped the grapefruit just like the lady had on the YouTube video she watched a few months ago.

"What's taking you so long, Cocoa? Got a nigga blindfolded looking crazy as fuck," O'Shea joked.

She walked back over to the bed and proceeded to give him the best head he had ever received. She had cut a hole in the grapefruit big enough so that his dick could fit snugly in. He gasped when she slid the warm grapefruit down his erection. Her hand, the grapefruit, and her mouth worked together simultaneously as he moaned, hissed, and bucked up off the bed. She had surely blessed the game and when he came it was amazing. Just like she'd always done, she swallowed every last drop of his release licking her lips afterward. He couldn't do anything but lay there and catch his breath as Kelsey went into the restroom and came out with a hot towel. She cleansed him thoroughly before trashing what was left of that poor grapefruit.

"Damn, that feels good," he whispered as she moved the towel from his shaft to his balls making sure to remove all the pulp from the fruit.

After removing the scarf from his eyes, she reached over to the table to get a condom and placed it on his thick erection. After all this time, she was beyond ready to feel him inside of her. This was her show, and she intended to keep the party going. O'Shea watched her intensely as she planted her feet firmly on each side of him and slowly lowered her body down onto his.

"Ahhh!" they both exclaimed once he filled her tight wet space. Kelsey kept her eyes closed unable to bring herself to look at him. His hips rose up off the bed, and they didn't move for a while wanting to savor the connection. Him being inside of her felt like a person coming home after years of living abroad. His dick was piping hot inside of her, and she loved the feel of it.

Kelsey began to move first, alternating rocking her hips and bouncing down on his dick. It felt so good that she threw her head back, her eyes rolling to the back of her head. She must have been moving too fast because he placed his hands on her waist forcing her to slow down. Kelsey wanted to fuck, and he was forcing her to make love. She wanted it rough and hard, but the things he was doing and saying to her had her feeling some type of way, a way she didn't want to feel.

"Look at me, Kelsey," he commanded.

"No," she replied and began contracting her walls squeezing his dick in an attempt to distract him.

"Please, Cocoa," he pleaded.

Kelsey did as she was asked, and when their eyes met, all she saw was their love strong as ever.

*Fuck, this may have been a mistake*, she thought and wondered if he could see through her just as she could see through him. Could he see the love she still had for him? Maybe he just saw the hurt that was there. The hurt that she continued to deny even existed.

O'Shea tilted his head and gave her a puzzled look that passed quickly. He lifted his hips and began stroking her tenderly, forcing the negative thoughts to the back of her mind where they belonged. He then rolled her over so that he was on top and made love to her like he had never done before. He sexed her like he was trying to prove a point, and she felt it in every single stroke, touch, lick, and kiss. Whatever he was doing, this was absolutely the best sex she had ever had in her life. She was no longer running the show because he was definitely the HNIC. He had her legs up in the air forming a peace sign as he tapped her spot repeatedly. Kelsey was in heaven.

After making love for hours, they got up to shower. O'Shea ordered some food, and they sat out on the terrace stuffing their faces wearing only their bath robes. He ordered pancakes, bacon, eggs, and was sure to get some mango and pineapple because he knew it was her favorite.

He stared at her as she bit a slice of pineapple and began to chew it slowly, closing her eyes.

"It's good, huh?" he asked.

"Yes, so good. You want some?" she asked offering him the rest of her slice. He nodded and took the remaining pineapple into his mouth along with her fingers and sucked them gently as she slowly pulled them out. She then placed those same fingers in her own mouth sucking the rest of the pineapple juice and his flavor from them. "Umm," she moaned causing his dick to twitch under his robe.

"Why you eat pineapple and mango so much?" For as long as he could remember, it had been one of her favorite snacks.

"I just love them, and plus, when I was younger, I heard my mom's homegirl Peaches telling her that eating pineapples and mango makes your kitty taste sweet," she replied, smiling naughtily.

"Get the fuck outta here! Really?" He burst out laughing. "That's why you taste so damn good?" he added, licking his own lips fienin' to taste her again…and that's just what he did. He pushed her robe out of his way and devoured her right there on the patio, making her cum again and again being sure he sucked and swallowed every drop of her nectar.

# Chapter Ten

O'Shea and Kelsey never even made it out of the room the first two days. They made love then showered, only to make love again, so the time flew by. They did manage to leave the room on their third day together to shop on Gloucester Avenue, float on the Martha Brae River, eat some of the most delicious food they had ever tasted, and dance in a club outside of the resort that night. It was the most fun either of them had had in a very long time, and it was even more special that they were doing it together.

In his suite lying in bed, Kelsey was on her cell phone checking her Instagram feed and loading up vacation pictures while O'Shea was on his laptop checking emails. She only posted pictures that didn't include him and some of the beautiful scenery in Jamaica. The pictures of them together she wanted to keep for her own personal collection. Kelsey didn't want people to think they were back together or anything, but she never wanted to forget the time they spent together either. Even without the pictures, the way he was handling her body guaranteed that every single moment would be embedded in her mind until the end of time. Kelsey had talked to her mother as well as Alana a few times since the trip, and they were both glad she was having a good time; however, she only told Alana that she was spending time with O'Shea. She was his biggest supporter and couldn't have been more thrilled, but Kelsey had to reel her friend in and let her know that she didn't need to get too hyped because this was only a vacation fling, and they were not getting back together.

During the trip, Kelsey ignored all but one of Melo's calls and regretted answering the one-time she did. She lied and said she wasn't getting good reception on her cell when he tried to throw a tantrum over her not checking in. She realized that she needed to break things off with him soon because he was behaving as if they were in a full-fledged relationship. If it wasn't so tacky, she would have told him over the phone that he could kick rocks, but she knew that would be childish of her, so she decided to wait until she returned home. Right now, she just wanted to enjoy the peace that she was feeling. They listened to the Weekend's station on Pandora, and the mood was super chill. O'Shea glanced over admiring his Cocoa Baby as she laid on her stomach messing with her phone without a stitch of clothing on. How was it that they weren't already married with babies? He never thought things would turn out this way. O'Shea couldn't remember the last time he felt this content and complete, but in just two days, it would be over. He would see her from time to time at a family function or hear of her accomplishments and life changes through his mother in passing, but that would be it. All he would be left with were the memories of their past. It was depressing just thinking about it. Kelsey looked up from her phone and noticed the look of dread on his face.

"Hey, you, what's going on in that head of yours?"

Deciding to be honest he said, "I'm just thinking that we only have two more days together. Really one full day since you fly out early Monday morning. I've enjoyed every moment of our time here, but I'm not gon' lie, I don't want it to end. I've missed you so much, Cocoa."

She appreciated his honesty but was not ready to tell him that she felt the same. It was just too much to deal with, and she wasn't ready to admit to him what she was feeling, let alone to herself. She had missed him too, but she couldn't go there with him. She was already dreading ending things with Melo when she returned home.

"Let's just make the most of the time we have left," she said as she climbed on top of his naked body kissing him tenderly on the lips. He took one of her nipples into his mouth and sucked it while he pinched and played with the other just like she liked. She was super wet, and he felt the puddle forming where she sat on his lower abdomen. He lifted her up and placed her directly on his erection.

"Aww, shit, Cocoa!" he shouted when he filled her up, "Yo' shit is so damn wet, baby."

She began moving up and down his pole causing his toes to curl something serious. She fucked him like this for a while, but when she brought her body down and grinded her pussy against him, she knew he was about to bust. It was also at that moment that they both realized he wasn't wearing a condom. They were skin to skin, and the shit felt wonderful. It was too late, and she couldn't stop even if she tried to. O'Shea hesitated, but Kelsey called out to him, "If you stop, Shea, I'm going to fucking kill you. I'm about to cum, baby!"

"Give it to me, Cocoa," he demanded as he tapped her spot repeatedly. She rocked her body against him once more, and it happened.

"Shea!" she screamed out as she came so hard that she squirted on his belly, triggering him to release inside of her. It felt like nothing neither of them had experienced before. When they were together before, they fucked raw from time to time, but he would pull out every time he came. Deep down, he selfishly hoped he had gotten her pregnant, so she would have no choice but to be in his life again. He knew it wasn't right, but he wanted her that bad. Knowing how careful Kelsey was though, she probably still took her birth control everyday like clockwork.

They laid there still connected trying to get their breathing under control. Kelsey made no attempt to get up, and he surely didn't want her to. After a while, O'Shea chuckled as a memory came to mind.

"Hey, Cocoa, you remember that time you broke up with a nigga for a whole week back in high school?" he asked causing them both to fall out laughing. O'Shea couldn't remember for the life of him why she cut him off, but he thought he was gone die when she did.

"Hell yeah, I remember," she said recalling a petty argument that caused her to tell him it was over, "I was so damn mad at you, Shea, but I can't remember exactly what you said. I'm not going to lie though, that was the longest week of my life. I missed your punk-ass like crazy. I was five minutes away from breaking down and calling you before you showed up at the house begging me to take you back. 'Oh, baby, baby please' looking-ass," Kelsey laughed, lifting her head to look up at him.

O'Shea couldn't help but laugh too because she wasn't telling no lies. She clowned his sad-ass for weeks after that shit. He didn't have any shame in his game though, and he would have said anything to get her to take him back. He just wanted his girl especially after seeing Kendrick trying to spark up a conversation with her at a track meet a few days after she dumped him. He tried to play that shit off, but he couldn't believe that she seemed to be straight without him and he was the one going insane with them being apart. The same thing could be said about how things were playing out with them now.

"What made you think about that?" she whispered, still smiling. Kelsey's head was now on his chest as he stroked her back gently. He could tell she was about to doze off.

"I don't know…" For a while, he didn't speak. Lost in his thoughts, trying to find the right words to say, he finally spoke up, "I guess the way that we both felt that week is how I've been feeling for the last two years. I've missed the fuck out of you, and I'm still in love with you, Cocoa."

When he didn't get a response from her, he assumed that she had fallen asleep. After staring up at the ceiling for a while, sleep finally found him, but Kelsey wasn't asleep though. She had heard every word O'Shea said but was unable to respond as a single tear escaped and slid down her face.

***

Kelsey was the first one up the following morning. She went to shower, leaving O'Shea asleep in the bed. She had enjoyed their time together tremendously and didn't want to it end just yet. A look of despair covered her face as she thought of saying goodbye to him the next day. She turned to her right side to look at his name tatted on her body and just stared at it wondering if she would ever get this man completely out of her system. When she finally emerged from the bathroom, he was awake, lying in bed staring off into space.

"Good morning."

"Morning, beautiful," he said looking her way.

"Hey, let's go to Kingston today," she said excitedly, "They have a bus that can get us there in no time."

"Sounds like a plan. I want to visit the *Bob Marley Museum*, but I ain't taking no fucking bus though. I'll have a car to take us there and back."

"Ok, big-time with your fancy-ass," she teased, making him laugh.

After wiping the sleep out of his eyes, Kelsey, who was already dressed, waited on him so they could head out. Once O'Shea was done taking a shower, he stood there in his boxers putting together his fit for the day.

"Shea, can I ask you a question?"

"Sure, you can ask me anything."

"What was it about her?"

He turned around to face her shocked that she would ask him that. "About who?" he asked, playing crazy.

"Shea, don't play." He knew damn well who she was talking about.

"Why you doing this now, Kels?" he asked, putting on his wife beater, "We're having such a good time."

This was a conversation that he never wanted to have with her. He always hoped that she didn't think him stepping out had anything to do with something she lacked. That wasn't the case at all. She just wasn't around enough.

"I'm not trying to ruin our good time, Shea. It's just something I've always wanted to know. After all this time, I wanted to ask you that, and you did just say that I could ask you anything."

"On the real, it had nothing to do with her, Kelsey. It was you. You started to act like you didn't need me anymore. You were never around, and I felt like I was no longer important to you. It wasn't something she had that you didn't. She just had time for a nigga and made me feel important."

"Shea, I had school. You have always known how I felt about you, and I've never given you a reason to doubt me. I always did whatever it was you wanted me to do. 'Stop cursing, Kelsey. It's not ladylike', 'Don't roll your eyes', 'Come to Baylor instead of Spelman like you dreamed of all your life, Kelsey', 'Don't do this, Kelsey, and don't do that, Kelsey'. The one time I didn't follow your rules, you started acting brand new."

O'Shea had never thought of it from her point of view. She made it seem as if he was running her life, and she couldn't make decisions for herself. He had never meant to make her feel like that. He only wanted to love and protect her, but instead he made her sacrifice who she was to meet his own standards. How did he even miss that? She was always so agreeable with any suggestions or demands he made. She was right. When she went against the grain, he turned on her and hadn't even realized it.

"How long were you messing with her?"

"To be very clear, I wasn't messing with her, Kelsey. I met her at the party Jamil threw after he was voted to the All-Star team. She ended up calling me a week later, and I asked her how she even got my number. She told me Jamil had given it to her. I told her I was in a relationship and thought that was the end of it, but she started texting, calling, and sending me pics and shit. I ignored her for a long time and thought about just changing my phone number, but then we got into it before you flew back to Dallas and I left for the away game against Atlanta. She texted that she was in Atlanta too and wanted to see me. That was the first and only time I responded to her. It only happened once, but as soon as it was over, I knew that I had made the biggest mistake of my life. I immediately told her that she needed to leave, and I went into the restroom and tried to call you, but you didn't pick up. I wanted to tell you the truth before you found out from someone else. Of course the girl was pissed and felt like I played her. She refused to leave and demanded that I take her to her hotel. The moment we stepped out of the Omni and saw all the cameras, I knew you were gone. I think she made the call to the paparazzi when I stepped out of the room to call you. I didn't understand how they knew exactly where we were. It's like I felt my whole heart break in half, but it was all on me. I haven't seen or spoken to 'ol girl since that day." O'Shea didn't even realize his tears were coming down until he looked up at her and noticed hers.

"I'm sure you know by now that I came home early from Dallas. I was at the house when the story broke," Kelsey said. She was upset with herself for even allowing him to see that what he had done still affected her this way, but it was time for the truth. When she left, she didn't allow him to give an explanation because there was nothing he could say at that time to ease her pain.

"Yeah, I thought I was going to have a heart attack when I came home and saw all your stuff gone."

"Shea, I came home to tell you that I was going part-time at work and taking a semester off from school because I didn't want to lose you. Too little too late, huh?" she asked attempting to wipe the tears from her face, but they continued to flow.

He didn't have shit to say. He didn't know that she planned to make those sacrifices for him, but he was glad that she didn't. After he broke her heart, she was forced to stand on her own and make decisions without him putting in his two cents. She was a better woman now because of it, and her departure from his life, honestly, made him a better man.

"Kelsey," he started to say, but she cut him off.

"I'm okay, Shea. I asked you for the truth, and I appreciate your honesty."

He hated that what he did still caused her pain to this day. If he could've rewound the hands of time, he would have surely done things differently.

"You know I've always loved you, right? That's one thing that has never changed, Cocoa."

"I know. Now let's get out of here and go have some fun," she said patting her eyes with some tissues.

\*\*\*

On Monday, O'Shea decided to ride with Kelsey to the airport then take the car back after he saw her off. They held hands and spoke very little on the ride there. They hadn't made love since the day before. At this point, it had nothing to do with sex. It was just about the time they spent together, and they had a great time. Kelsey cracked jokes, and O'Shea laughed more than he had in a while, just like old times. A five-mile run on the beach, diving at Widow Makers Cove, eating more marvelous food, and drinking rum until they were both completely wasted was how they spent their last day and night together.

At the airport, Kelsey stepped out of the car first, and he followed closely behind to retrieve her luggage from the trunk.

"Give me five minutes," he told the driver, closing the door.

"Kelsey, I….," he stumbled trying to find the right words to say to her.

"Just kiss me, Shea. This doesn't have to be that difficult," she half-smiled looking just as lost as he felt.

He kissed her lips gently and looked into her eyes deciding that he had to be honest with her about his feelings because he didn't know if he would ever get another chance again, so he held her close as he spoke.

"I had a fantastic time with you this past week, Cocoa. To have shared this experience with you has meant the world to me. An amazing five days with a person who I've considered my best friend and the love of my life since I can remember. Now I know what we initially agreed to, but I want it all. I want you back in my life…forever. I know I messed things up before, and I could never tell you how sorry I am for that. You said that you've forgiven me, but I don't know if that's entirely true. I just hope that one day you truly will. One thing I learned this week is that you were made just for me and me for you. I'm not speaking just about the sex, which is off the damn hook by the way. Our history, the chemistry, the conversations, but most of all our love, all of it, all of you, I believe, was made just for me, and the way I feel about you I ain't ever felt for anyone else. I know for a fact that I never will because you are it for me. Give me a chance to show you that I'm better. I promise to never hurt you again, Kels," he pleaded.

"O'Shea…," she started.

He saw the confusion as well as the love in her eyes as he spoke. She loved him but was too afraid to even consider what he was asking her.

"You might not feel the same way, and I'm sorry for flipping the script on you like this. Don't answer me now. Take as much time as you need. I've waited two years for this chance, so I'll continue to wait as long as it takes. I love you, Cocoa Baby," he said stroking the side of her face. He kissed her one last time before hopping back in the car on his way back to the resort for two more days. O'Shea didn't believe that is was a mere coincidence that they came to the same place for vacation. He believed in his heart that it was God's way of bringing them back together, and he was willing to do whatever it took to make them a reality again.

Kelsey stood there stunned, unable to move after O'Shea's car pulled away from the curb. Part of her wanted to hail a cab and follow him back to the resort and tell him she loved him too and wanted all the same things he wanted, but the other part told her to run as far away from him as she could. How could she trust him after he hurt her the way he had?

*I'd be a fool to go back after that, right?*

Her ringing cell phone broke Kelsey out of her trance. It was her mother calling to see if she was already on the plane. She informed her that she would be boarding soon and that she would call her as soon as she landed. Kelsey had to take care of the situation with Melo before she even thought about responding to O'Shea's admission of everlasting love. Shaking her head, she made her way inside the airport.

# Chapter Eleven

*I* *don't know how I let them talk me into coming to play bingo*, Kelsey thought, smiling as she dabbed the next number that appeared on the monitor on her cards. She had been in a bad mood all week but had to admit that she was having a good time with her mother and Vickie today. Vickie had already won $750, and her mother won a 32-inch television in a raffle. Everyone there seemed to know one another very well and cracked plenty of jokes keeping her entertained. She returned from Jamaica a week ago and hadn't said much about her trip, so Anita decided to get Kelsey out of the house for some fun. Eventually she let on that she knew O'Shea had been there too, but she didn't press Kelsey for any details about what went down between them while they were there. Since returning home, Kelsey had not been able to catch up with Melo due to his busy schedule, but they planned to have dinner at her home the following evening.

The first round of bingo ended, and she decided to stick around for the next session. "Ms. Vickie, how you been?" she asked noticing that she was coughing frequently.

*Maybe she's coming down with something*, Kelsey thought.

"I'm okay, baby, just can't seem to shake this cough."

It was then that Kelsey noticed the changes in Vickie's appearance. She looked as if she has lost about fifteen pounds, and she looked so tired. She had always been a petite woman, so the weight loss was very noticeable. Something just didn't feel right.

"How was your doctor's appointment a few weeks back? What did Dr. Fisher say about that cough?" she asked becoming very concerned.

"It went okay. He gave me some cough syrup."

Kelsey heard her mother suck her teeth, making her look back and forth between the two women. Vickie was shushing Anita with her eyes, so Kelsey made a mental note to ask her mother about it later. Her nursing experience coupled with the way the two women were behaving let her know something serious was going on with Vickie.

"Well, make sure you call him if that cough persists. He might want to do a few scans." She was aware of Ms. Vickie's breast cancer history, but after chemo, radiation, and surgery, she had been in remission for some time.

"I sure will, baby girl. Don't be worrying about me. I'll be just fine." Kelsey looked at Anita who was now shaking her head wearing a weary expression on her face. Something was definitely going on, and Kelsey planned on finding out exactly what it was.

$500 in winnings later, she was glad she decided to stay for the second session and was now on her way home to chill thinking about how dinner with Melo would go tomorrow. He was super cool, and it was going to be hard ending things with him, but it was necessary. She was never going to be ready for what he wanted, and she knew that now. He deserved much more, and until she was completely over O'Shea, no other guy stood a chance. She was only home for about an hour when she got a call from her mother saying that she needed to come to the hospital because Vickie had collapsed while they were shopping. An ambulance was called, and she was being transported to the hospital. Kelsey rushed over right away. She knew something wasn't right with her when they were together earlier. After arriving at the hospital and learning of Ms. Vickie's condition from her oncologist, Kelsey broke down. Her cancer had returned and metastasized, taking a toll on her body. Vickie declined another round of chemo and radiation months ago which at this point would only prolong the inevitable. She knew she was dying and had made peace with it. She just wanted to enjoy what little time she had left with her friends and family. Vickie was like a second mother to Kelsey, and it hurt her terribly to think that one day very soon she would be gone.

*Oh, my God, what about O'Shea?* He was extremely close to his mother, and she knew this was going to be hard on him.

"Mom, has anyone contacted Shea to let him know what's going on? Do you know if Ms. Vickie even discussed with him what's about to happen?" Kelsey asked in a shaky voice.

"No, baby, I haven't called him yet. She wanted to tell him in person and planned to once he came to visit her this coming week."

"Ok, well, I'm calling him. I know he would want to be here with her right now." She stepped out into the hallway, placing the call to O'Shea.

"Hello."

"Hey, Shea, it's Kelsey."

"Damn, hey, Kels. It's so crazy that you called right now because I was just thinking about you as I was getting off the plane." She had been on his mind constantly, and he didn't even leave his room for the two remaining days that he was in Jamaica. He was too depressed. Her departure took a lot out of him.

"Where are you right now?"

"I just landed in Dallas. I came a few days early to see Ma."

"Thank God you're already here. Look, Shea, I need you to come to St. Paul before you go anywhere else, okay?" She knew it was no one but God that brought him there. If he would have waited like he originally planned to, there was a possibility that he may not have been able to say goodbye to his mother.

"What's going on, Kelsey? Are you okay?" He began to panic.

"Not really, but I would rather not talk about it over the phone. Just get here now."

"I'm on my way." They hung up, and she texted him where he could find her once he got to the hospital.

He rushed through the airport and out to the car awaiting him, instructing his driver to get him to the hospital quickly. He was anxious and thought maybe his mother could fill him in on what was going on. He called her at home and on her cell but got no answer. He didn't know what was going on, but he couldn't shake the bad feeling in the pit of his stomach.

At the hospital, Kelsey ran into Melo as he was making rounds on the Oncology unit with some of his colleagues. He noticed her sitting in the waiting area and excused himself to go and speak to her.

"Kelsey, baby, what are you doing here?"

"Hey, Melo, Ms. Vickie was brought in a few hours ago, and she's not doing too well," she told him as the tears slid down her face. He reached out and pulled her close, comforting her as she continued to explain everything that had happened. He hugged her tight knowing how much Vickie meant to her and her mother.

O'Shea exited the elevator as the two were embracing. *At least she's okay*, he thought. On the way over, he pictured all of the terrible things that could have happened to land Kelsey in the hospital, but it was obvious she wasn't the reason he had been summoned there.

"Hey, Kels...I'm here now, so tell me what's going on," he said interrupting their moment.

"Melo, will you excuse us?"

He released her and kissed her forehead. "Sure, I'm going to finish up my rounds, but I'll come back to check on you later, okay?"

She nodded and grabbed O'Shea by his hand, leading him in the direction of his mother's room. Vickie woke up about twenty minutes ago and was talking and laughing with Anita like nothing had ever happened when the pair walked in.

"Ma, what's going on? Why didn't you tell me you were in the hospital?" he asked making his way over to her side taking note of how much weight she had lost since he'd last seen her.

"Hug my neck first, son, then have a seat, and I'll answer all of your questions."

He did as he was told as tears already clouded his vision. He knew that whatever his mother was about to tell him wasn't good. Kelsey and Anita left the room to give them some privacy. Mentally exhausted from the day's events, they decided to go to the cafeteria for some coffee.

"Mom, why don't you go on home and get some rest? I'll hang out and make sure Vickie and Shea are okay."

Anita was hesitant at first but finally agreed. "I need to stop by my manager's office first to request some time off. Vickie needs me, and I intend to be there for her," she stated sadly. Kelsey hugged her mother tightly feeling bad that she was about to lose her best friend of more than thirty years.

When Kelsey returned to the waiting area, she found O'Shea sitting in a chair with his head in his hands. She stopped and just studied him for a moment having no idea what she could say to make him feel better, so she decided to do the only thing she could do and that was to be there for him.

"Shea," she called to him softly.

When he looked up at her, the pain etched in his face was evident, and it broke her heart. She kneeled before him and wrapped her arms around his neck. O'Shea hugged her back with his face in her neck, crying silently. No sounds came from him, but she felt the wetness of his tears against her skin.

"Come on, let's get you together before you go back in there to see her. It will break her heart to see you like this. She is going to need you to be strong, Shea."

"I can't take this, Kels. I don't think I'm strong enough," he said unable to contain his emotions.

"You are strong enough, and when you can't be, I got you. Now, let's go back in there and spend some time with Ms. Vickie," she said cleaning his face with the napkins she held.

He was so thankful for Kelsey and didn't know how he would've made it through this without her. He nodded and followed her back to his mother's room where they stayed for the next few hours talking until she fell asleep on them.

"Where are you staying while you're in Dallas?" she asked.

"I was going to stay at the house with Ma, but now, I'll probably just check into a hotel."

She stood up and held her hand out to him. "Come on, you can crash at my place."

"I don't know, Kelsey," he said unsure of where they stood after their time together in Jamaica. It was clear that she was still involved with Melo, and he had enough to deal with right now. Whatever they had going on had to be put in the back of his mind for now.

"Come on, Shea, fuck all that other shit you thinking about. I know you don't want to be alone right now, and we're family before anything else. This ain't about nothing but me being here for you like you would be for me. Like I said earlier, 'I got you.'" He took her hand, and they headed out after he kissed his sleeping mother's forehead. She was taking some pretty heavy pain medication and would probably be out until he returned the following morning.

\*\*\*

"Dope ride," O'Shea said once they were seated inside her brand new Mercedes-Benz G Class SUV. That was another gift she gave herself after graduating.

"I know right," she said lightweight bragging. She'd only had it for a few weeks, but she really loved her new whip.

It took them less than ten minutes to arrive at her place uptown. Once inside, he was very impressed to say the least. Her condo was the shit and was beautifully decorated. It was bachelorette pad for sure. During the tour, he looked at her sideways when he saw the stripper pole her hot ass had installed in her huge bedroom. Yeah, his Cocoa Baby had definitely changed on him. He was hoping that one day he would be able to see her slide down that bitch and put on a show just for him.

"Are you hungry?"

"Starving," he replied remembering that he hadn't had anything to eat all day.

"You still like breakfast for dinner?"

"You know it," he said flattered that she remembered.

"Take your things into the guest room. You'll find everything you need stored in the cabinet in the restroom. Get cleaned up, and the food will be ready when you come back."

"Thanks, Kelsey, I appreciate you letting me stay here."

"No problem, Shea," she smiled as he walked away. She prepared pancakes, turkey bacon, turkey sausage links, eggs, cheesy grits, along with some fresh pineapple and mango. By the time O'Shea emerged from the guest room fresh and clean, everything was done as promised.

"Damn, Kels, you didn't have to do all this," he said more than impressed. His stomach growled at the sight of the food.

"Don't worry about all that. Come sit down, and I'll fix your plate."

As he made his way over to the island to dig in, Kelsey couldn't help but notice how good he looked wearing a simple tank and some basketball shorts. She had to make herself focus on her food several times to keep her eyes from roaming all over him.

Everything was absolutely delicious. "I'm gone have to put in extra work to burn off that meal," he said sitting back with his hand on his stomach.

"In that case, we can hit Katy Trail and get a few miles in tomorrow morning before heading back to the hospital."

"I knew better than to say that shit out loud," he complained.

"Stop being a cry baby, Shea. A few miles ain't gone hurt your ass," she laughed.

"As long as it's just a few, Cocoa. You know how you do," he fussed. She laughed because he always hated running with her and complained that she didn't know when to stop. He used to fuss about it all the time. It felt good being in his presence again. She just hated the circumstances that brought them back together.

The way his eyes scanned her from head to toe caused her to become nervous.

"Hey, why don't you put in a DVD while I jump in the shower real quick?" she said quickly exiting the kitchen.

"What do you want to watch?" he called behind her tickled by her quick escape.

"You know what I like," she called over her shoulder before closing her bedroom door.

*She don't have to be nervous around me*, he thought, *I won't bite unless she asks me to.*

Kelsey took her time in the shower, trying to wash away all her worries. *Poor Ms. Vickie.* She had always admired the relationship she had with God and knew as well as Vickie did where she was going when she transitioned from this life to the next. Kelsey's tears mixed with the water that ran down her face thinking of how much she would miss her. She also cried for the loss of her brother years before and how O'Shea helped her through that difficult time in her life, and she planned to do the same for him now. Her brother's death was so unexpected but having the advantage of knowing Vickie would go soon didn't make it any easier. The pain was still the same.

When she finally returned to the living room, he had season one of *Martin* playing and was already cracking up laughing. He looked up to see her dressed simply in her favorite Old Navy pajama bottoms and a white tank top. She noticed that he'd already poured her a cup of her favorite wine and grabbed himself a beer. The kitchen was clean, and the food had been put away.

*This nigga here sure knows what to do*, she thought to herself.

Looking back at the television, she laughed at old man Otis whooping ass and plopped down on the couch next to Shea.

"This is one of my favorite episodes," she said as she sipped her wine.

"I know," he said moving his eyes from her back to the television. His face suddenly turned serious as he sat his beer down and leaned back resting his head on the couch pillows. "Cocoa, what am I supposed to do without my mom? All my life it's just been me and her. Shit's fucked up, baby."

"It is fucked up, Shea, but you're not alone. Remember when KJ passed?"

"Yeah," he said remembering his little homie.

"I didn't think the pain of losing him would ever go away. Sometimes I still cry when I think about what he would be doing right now if he was still alive. I miss that boy something terrible, but it got easier over time. If it wasn't for you, I don't think I would have been able to handle it as well as I did. You will never know what that meant to me, Shea. I plan to be here for you just like you were for me, and you know my moms will always be there too, not to mention the rest of both of our families. I told you I got you, Shea. We got you," she said as she nudged him softly.

"I know you do, and I love you for that."

"I love you too," she replied resting her head on his shoulder, letting his arm drape around her. They remained quiet and continued to watch the DVD until they both drifted off to sleep.

Kelsey woke up the next morning curled up in Shea's lap with her head resting on his chest. She looked up to find him staring at her. No matter what position they were in when they went to sleep, when they woke up, she would always be laying with her head on his chest.

*Old habits die hard,* she thought.

"Good morning," he smiled.

"Good morning to you too. Did you sleep any?" she asked him wiping sleep from her eyes.

"A little bit," he replied. Mostly, he watched her and prayed for his mother.

"Come on, and let's get that run in before we head back up to the hospital."

"Damn, I was hoping you would've forgot," he whined. He wasn't really up to it but was willing to go just to please her.

"Uhhh, yeah, and don't try flaking on me either. Get dressed and give me about ten minutes."

"Ok." He grabbed her hand before she could walk off. "Thanks again for last night, Cocoa. I really didn't want to be alone."

"No problem," she said as she gently squeezed his hand before making her way to her room. She picked up her cell and discovered that Melo had texted and called her numerous times throughout the night.

*I'll holla at him later,* she thought before quickly dressing for her run with Shea.

# Chapter Twelve

Whand other family members from both the hospital, Anita sides were already there, and to Kelsey's surprise, Melo was there as well. He was shocked to see her walk in with Shea, and it showed all over his face. She walked over to greet him as Shea continued on to his mother's room.

"Kelsey, what's going on? I called you last night to make sure you were good but didn't get an answer," he said not hiding his irritation with her.

"I know you called, Romelo. I saw the missed calls when I woke up this morning, and I planned to get in contact with you later. When I left here last night, I went home, showered, and went to sleep." She was unsure why she was even explaining herself to him. What she did was her damn business.

"Are you sure that's all that happened?"

"What the fuck are you talking about?" Kelsey asked raising her voice clearly confused with his line of questioning.

He pulled her to the side after a few family members began to look in their direction. Her cousin Nate even stood up and looked at Melo with a serious mean mug. He knew not to fuck with Kelsey with him around, so he calmed himself down before he continued in a low voice.

"What I'm talking about is the fact that I saw you leaving here last night with your ex, you don't bother answering my calls or texts all night, and then you show up here with him this morning. What would you think if you were me?"

"I really don't care what you think happened. I told you what it was and that's what the hell it is, and I really don't appreciate what it is that you're accusing me of, but I don't feel the need to even explain myself to you either. That's not the type of relationship we have. Am I right?"

"Right, but…"

"Look, this is not the time nor place for this. My family is going through something right now, so we can discuss this later," Kelsey said beyond pissed.

"Fair enough," he replied defeated. He was becoming tired of her calling all the shots in their relationship. He wanted to be with her exclusively and planned on having a serious conversation with her when the time was right. Not getting his way wasn't something he was used to. He always got what he wanted, and Kelsey was who he wanted. Nearly a year of kicking it, and he was no closer to getting her to commit than he had been in the beginning. He had a feeling O'Shea Lewis was a huge part of the problem.

*** 

The family had finally all gone home, so Kelsey went in to see Vickie. Melo left about an hour before but only after she agreed to have dinner with him later. When he was there, he seemed to be trying to let everyone know she was his girl, and it was ticking her off, holding her hand, kissing her cheek, and sticking by her side especially when Shea was around. She only agreed to dinner so that she could finally break things off with his petty-ass. This shit had gone on long enough.

"There's my girl," Vickie said as Kelsey entered her room, "Where you been, baby?"

"Waiting for everyone to leave. I won't stay long. I know you must be tired."

"Yeah, boo, I am tired."

"Are you in any pain, Ma?"

"Not right now. This Morphine drip is doing the trick. I told O'Shea I wanted to go home, so he's talking to Dr. Fisher and the case manager about home hospice."

"Thank you, Ms. Vickie," Kelsey said out of nowhere.

"For what, baby?"

"Just for being you and always being there for me. I feel like I was blessed with two mothers in my life. You've been such an inspiration to me, and I'm really going to miss you. I love you so much."

At this point, they were both crying. "I love you too, baby. You know my son is still in love with you, right?" She shushed Kelsey with her finger raised before she could respond. "And I believe that you are still in love with him too. Am I right?"

Kelsey only nodded, unable to speak. There was no need to front, and she would never lie to Vickie anyway.

"I know he hurt you bad before, but he's learned from his mistakes. Losing you almost broke him. Trust me…I know. Life is short, Kelsey, and it's rare that folks find what you two have. One day, you're here, and the next, you're gone." After a short coughing spell and a sip of the water that Kelsey offered her, Vickie continued. "Kelsey, it makes no sense to not spend the short time we have on earth with the person we love especially when you know for a fact that person truly loves you too. Now, if he fucks up again, you walk away and don't look back. I don't give a damn if he is my son." They both laughed. "Look after my boy, okay?" she said with tears in her eyes.

"Always," Kelsey promised. They embraced with tears flowing down their faces. She released Vickie and fluffed her pillows and adjusted her covers trying to make her as comfortable as possible.

O'Shea stood on the other side of the door and watched through the glass as his two favorite ladies in the world talked oblivious that he was even there. When O'Shea wasn't in the room visiting with his mother, he sat back in the waiting area and watched how Kelsey interacted with her god daughter Kennedi. She was great with her and hoped that one day she would get to experience motherhood firsthand even if it wasn't with him. Kelsey was a natural, and he could tell that Kennedi loved her dearly. Right then and there, he decided to claim it— Kelsey would one day be his wife and the mother of his children.

"Hey, Ma, you ready to go home?" O'Shea asked finally walking into the room.

"Yeah, baby, I'm ready." She wiped Kelsey's tears and then her own.

"Ok, everything has been arranged, and I'll be here in Dallas as long as you need me," he said kissing her cheek.

\*\*\*

Dinner with Melo turned out to be a disaster after 'ol boy ended up throwing a mild temper tantrum. How dare Kelsey break up with him? It was time for dessert, and that's when things went left. They met up at Morton's uptown and enjoyed drinks and dinner. Everything was going good at first until he tried it by laying out how things needed to change in order for them to move forward in their relationship.

"Look, Kelsey, we've been seeing each other for almost a year now, and I really dig everything about you. We have a great time outside and inside of the bedroom; although, the latter is where our relationship began. I admit that I knew what the deal was when we first started hanging out, and it was cool for a minute, but the more time I spent with you, the more I wanted out of what we have going on. From the jump, you've been in control of every aspect of our relationship, but I think I deserve to have a say in where we go from here," he said confidently.

"And where do you think we go from here, Romelo?" she asked just to see where the conversation was heading.

"I want you to give us a real chance, Kelsey. I want exclusivity and for us to actually be working toward something real."

"I'm so sorry, Melo, but I can't give you what you're asking for," she answered truthfully.

"You can't?" he asked slightly taken aback.

"No, I can't."

"Is it because of him?" There was no need to beat around the bush. They both knew the "him" he was referring to.

"Yes and no. My relationship with O'Shea is what it is, Romelo. Before we were together, we were friends, more like family, and nothing or no one can break the bond that we have. If you and I were in a serious relationship, would you be comfortable with me being friends with O'Shea knowing the history we have?"

"Honestly, I wouldn't be, Kelsey. I would expect you to be respectful of our relationship."

"There's nothing wrong with feeling that way, and I don't think there is a man who would be able to deal with the friendship Shea and me share, and I wouldn't expect them to either, but no man will ever be able to tell me that I can't be friends with him or talk to him regardless of what went down between us."

"He wasn't too much of a friend to do what he did to you, Kelsey. I can't believe that you're choosing that cheater over me," he said with a look of contempt.

"That's one of the reasons you and I could never go any further, Melo. You're worried about the wrong shit. It's none of your business what happened between me and Shea. That was between us, and it has absolutely nothing to do with you. I don't need your approval to forgive him. I think the issue you really have is that you're not used to being told no."

"What the hell does that mean?" he asked clearly offended.

"What I mean, Romelo, is that you're extremely attractive, successful, great in bed, and despite being a spoiled brat, you're fun to kick it with. Basically the total package, right? So how dare I turn down your suggestion to take our relationship to the next level? Any other female would have jumped at the chance to be with you. You're a good catch and you know it, so how could I not want to be with you?"

"Exactly," he replied. Romelo wasn't trying to sound arrogant at all but was sure of himself and what he had to offer her. "But you don't want me?" he asked annoyed.

"No, Romelo, I don't, not in the way a woman should want a man who she plans to build a life with. My heart is still with someone else, so I could never give you what you need," she admitted to him and finally to herself.

"You know what? Fuck it, Kelsey," he said as he opened his wallet and threw a few bills down on the table to cover their dinner, "Keep chasing after a dude who cheated on you for the world to see. He's probably just gonna fuck you over again, and when he does, you'll be wishing you gave us a chance. Hell, you should be glad a black man in my position ever wanted to be with you in the first place and not some white woman," he said with his voice slightly raised.

"And there it is! I've been wondering what else it was that was holding me back, and now I've finally figured it out," she laughed as she clapped her hands.

"And what is it that you think you've figured out?"

"I wasn't trying to hurt your feelings, but here it is, Romelo. Even if Shea wasn't in the picture, I could never be with a man who thinks he's better than me. Someone who thinks I should feel lucky being with him, like you're some fucking prize. A white woman can have your ass, baby, because I don't want you. You stay in your feelings worse than a female does, and that's some shit I could never get with. Now go on and leave before you embarrass yourself any further."

Romelo just shook his head, disgusted with her before he walked away.

*What a fucking cry baby!* she thought. Kelsey felt a smidge bad for him, but he knew what it was off the muscle. *Ain't my fault that his ass caught feelings.*

Kelsey enjoyed the rest of her dessert and ignored the stares from those around her after witnessing Romelo's departure.

# Chapter Thirteen

A little over two weeks later, Ms. Vickie passed away in her home surrounded by family and friends. Kelsey and her mother spent lots of time with her and O'Shea in the weeks leading up to her death. Anita handled all of the funeral arrangements, so that O'Shea didn't have to. Vickie shared with her how she wanted things to be, and Anita was more than happy to carry out the final wishes of her dearest friend. As promised, Kelsey was right by O'Shea's side throughout it all. During those two weeks, he would either come by after she got off work, or she would go visit him at Ms. Vickie's and help him pack up her belongings. They would chill and talk, but a lot of times, they sat in silence just needing to be near one another. Kelsey held onto his hand at the memorial service, and she couldn't tell who was squeezing tighter. She just wanted to reassure him that she was there for him and always would be.

A little before the service was over, Kelsey noticed her father sitting all the way in the back of the church. She almost didn't recognize him. She had to admit that he looked good, just like his old self, but she fidgeted in her seat uncomfortable by his presence. O'Shea looked over at her with concern, but Kelsey just responded with a smile.

*Maybe he got his life back on track*, she thought as she squeezed his hand even tighter.

Although, deep down, she was happy for her father, she still wanted nothing to do with him. Attempting to be cordial, Anita spoke, but Kelsey avoided him completely.

\*\*\*

Two weeks later, Kelsey pulled out a box from her storage closet and began packing up Romelo's things. Despite his outburst at Morton's, he had been calling her everyday trying to get her to see things his way. Kelsey wasn't trying to hear that shit though, but she knew she couldn't avoid him any longer when he called and asked if it was okay for him to stop by and pick up some things he'd left at her place. All she could find were a few clothes, a tooth brush, some medical journals, and a few other insignificant items. To her, they were all things that he could have easily replaced, so she figured that this was just another excuse for him to come over. He had another thing coming though if he thought he was gone get some 'goodbye-pussy' from her.

Quickly packing everything neatly in a box, she waited for him to arrive as her mind drifted off to the fact that she hadn't heard from Shea all day. He would be leaving for LA the following morning, and she was really hoping they would have an opportunity to talk about their relationship before he left.

*Knock. Knock. Knock.*

The knocking at her front door broke Kelsey out of her thoughts of him. Taking a deep breath, she opened the door for Romelo with the box already in her hand. She had no intention of inviting him in.

"Romelo…," she said with no emotion, handing him his stuff as he stood there. She could tell he wanted to say something, but whatever it was, he could say that shit outside.

"How you been, Kelsey?" he asked clearly stalling.

"Fine," she replied hoping to keep the conversation short and sweet.

*Damn, she's not even going to invite me in?* he thought to himself. He was hoping to smash one more time while he was there, but it didn't seem like she was going for that, so he began rummaging through the box and found his ticket inside.

"Hey, I don't see my shaving kit in here. I put it under the sink in your restroom," he told her. He had another one at home and really didn't need it but was doing whatever he could to get on the other side of her door.

"I forgot about that. Come on in, and I'll grab it for you." Kelsey really didn't want him in her house but decided that being rude wasn't necessary.

No sooner than she went into her room, there was another knock at the door. Melo looked out the peep hole to see O'Shea standing on the other side with a smile on his face. Kelsey obviously hadn't heard him knock, so Melo thought he would have a little fun with her guest. He quickly removed his shirt and unbuckled his pants. When he opened the door, the smile that was plastered on O'Shea's face was quickly replaced with an angry scowl. For a second, Melo thought he had made a mistake by playing games with the baller because he looked as if he was about to beat his ass, and Melo wasn't really about that life. He was a pretty boy who had never been in a fight. He went to private schools all his life, and the white kids were afraid of him for no other reason than the fact that he was black.

"Hey, man, you here to see Kelsey? She's in bed but let me grab her real quick," he offered. He was hoping and praying that she didn't walk out and bust him in front of her ex.

"No, man, don't worry about it. It's clear that I stopped by at a bad time. Will you just let her know that I came by?" O'Shea asked looking heartbroken. Here he was coming by to tell her goodbye and to find out where they stood, and she was in there doing her thing with the next nigga. It was clear that she wasn't interested in giving him another chance.

"You sure, man? I'm telling you it's not a problem," he offered again sounding fake as hell.

"Yeah, I'm positive," O'Shea said before walking away shaking his head. Melo could only laugh at the poor guy. Now O'Shea knew what it felt like to be dismissed, just like Kelsey had done to him.

Melo closed the door and turned around just as Kelsey was coming out of her bedroom. He didn't know what took her so long but was relieved that she didn't walk in before O'Shea left. She had double checked to make sure she collected everything that belonged to Melo so that he would never have any excuse to come back. She was done playing games, and she knew who she wanted in her life—O'Shea Ramone Lewis. What she didn't expect to find when she walked out into her living room was a shirtless, pants half down Melo.

"Romelo, what the hell do you think you're doing? Put your clothes on. I can assure you that ain't shit going down with us tonight or any other night for that matter," she spat. She didn't even give him a chance to respond before she picked up his shirt, threw it in the box, and escorted him out of her door.

"Kelsey, wait…," he started to say, but she cut him off.

"Save it, Romelo. I really don't want to hear anything you have to say right now. Have a nice life and lose my fucking number," she yelled as she shoved his to-go box in his hands before slamming the door in his face. She immediately called down to the front desk and had his name removed from the list of guests who could come up to her place without the attendant having to call up for approval first. After ending the call, she placed another one to O'Shea, but he didn't answer, so she left a message and hoped to hear back from him before his flight the next day.

In the hallway, Romelo was busy putting his shirt back on and getting himself together. Although he didn't get what he came for, he was satisfied knowing that neither did O'Shea. With that comforting thought, he left his box of random items right where it was in the hallway and walked away. He didn't know why he was having such a hard time letting go. He had never been this pressed behind a female, but Kelsey had his head gone. Maybe this was karma getting him back for all the women he'd done wrong over the years. He was doing petty shit that he had never done before just to get next to her, and that was out of character for him. He knew it was over, and at this point, he made the choice to finally move on.

***

Kelsey was hurt that O'Shea returned to LA without even saying goodbye, and he never brought up what he said to her in Jamaica.

*Maybe he changed his mind*, she thought.

He was going through a lot, and their relationship was probably the furthest thing from his mind, so she didn't bring it up while he was in town. She was tired of racking her brain trying to figure out what was going on with him, so she decided to get out of the house. Kelsey had the day off and was bored to death, so she hit her mother up to see if she wanted to go to play bingo. Anita didn't answer either, but since Kelsey was in the area, she decided to just stop by. There was a car that she didn't recognize parked in the driveway, so she assumed her mother had company.

"Let me find out this lady done found her a man after all these years", she laughed to herself.

As far as she knew, her mother hadn't dated since her father left back in the day, and if she did have a man, she never brought anyone around. Kelsey knocked, but when she didn't get an answer, she used her key to let herself in.

"Mom," she called out but got no response.

She looked around the house and couldn't find her mother, so she pulled out her phone to dial her number but stopped when she heard voices coming from the backyard. Kelsey walked over and stared out of the sliding patio glass where she found her mother and father sitting, drinking sweet tea, and talking. They even seemed to be enjoying each other's company.

*Is this not the same man who abandoned his family for the streets? How could she have him all up in her house like shit is sweet?*

"Hey, Mom, I've been calling you...," Kelsey said as she slid the door open making her presence known. Not expecting to see her, Anita was caught off guard.

"I'm sorry, baby. My phone is inside, and I didn't hear it ringing."

"Hello, Kelsey," her father said.

"Father," she replied hella annoyed.

"How have you been, baby girl?" he asked.

"Please don't call me that, and I have been doing just fine. If you would've been around, you would already know that. Look, Mom, I'll come back when your company leaves" she said before sliding the door closed.

Kelvin Sr. looked to Anita for help, but she turned her head and sipped her tea. She refused to get in the middle of their father-daughter issues. Just because she forgave him didn't mean Kelsey had, and he would need to repair that relationship himself, so he got up and followed her out of the house, catching up with her before she made it back to her truck.

"Kelsey, wait just a second. We need to talk," he pleaded.

She turned around and mean mugged the shit out of her father. "What is so important that we got to talk right now after all this time? Do you know how many times I wanted to talk to you? How many things I wanted to share with *my* father? You weren't there for me then, but I'm supposed to listen to what you have to say now? What could you possibly want to talk to me about?" she yelled as her eyes misted.

Kelvin just stood there for a minute unsure of where to begin. He loved his family. His wife was his life, and although, they were young when they met, they were deeply in love. They struggled terribly after having the kids, and he had a hard time finding work. Instead of continuing to grind it out, he turned to drugs and alcohol. Anita was holding it down as best she could, going to school and working full time, but he felt like a complete failure. When the drugs got hold of him though, he was too embarrassed to stay. For years, he was in and out of jail for robbery and drug charges. After one of his many releases, he learned from his cousin that his only son Kelvin Jr. had been killed in a car accident a few months before. Because he made a point to stay away from his friends and family, no one knew how to get in contact with him when his boy died. He became extremely depressed and fell even deeper into drugs and drinking, but he got clean with the help of a church group that came out in the community to help homeless people and drug addicts. They saved his life, and now he wanted a second chance to right his wrongs with his family.

"I want to start off by telling you how sorry I am for walking out on you, Kelsey. It was a coward move, but I was just too ashamed of what I had become to stick around. I also want you to know how much I love you. I never stopped loving you, your mother, or your brother. I will never know what the full impact of not having me around had on your life, and I don't think I will ever forgive myself for that," he told his daughter.

"I don't know if I can either. We needed you. I mean you didn't even show up when KJ died." Her tears began to fall. "I went from being a daddy's girl to not having a daddy at all. I looked for you every day wondering if you would ever come back. How could you do that to me?"

"I don't know what to say, Kelsey. Because of my addiction, I separated myself from my entire family, and I found out that KJ died after I got out of jail and ran into my cousin Donnie. He told me that my son had been gone for months, and I had no idea. I felt like the scum of the earth for not being there. I knew at that point I could never come back, and my addiction only got worse. I have my shit together now, Kelsey, and I wouldn't be here if I didn't. I don't know if you will ever want me to be a part of your life, and I can't blame you if you don't. I don't deserve a second chance to be your dad, but I'm asking for one anyway," he said desperately.

"I don't know..." Kelsey didn't know if she could trust him again. He had been everything to her as a child, and when he left, she was crushed.

"Can I at least hug you before you go?" She simply nodded as he approached her with tears in his eyes too. "I love you so much, Kelsey Marie, and you are still the most beautiful girl I have ever seen. I am so proud of the woman that you have grown up to be and all you have accomplished," he said as he embraced his only daughter. This made her smile. This was the father she remembered, always telling her how beautiful and smart she was.

"Thanks. I have to go, but can you tell Mom that I'll call her later?"

"Sure."

"Dad?"

"Yes, baby girl," he answered happy to hear her call him that.

"You can get my number from Mom and call me sometime if you want."

"I will. Take care of yourself, Kelsey."

\*\*\*

When Kelsey made it home, she called to see if Alana was home. Today had been emotional to say the least, and she needed to talk to someone. She wished she could call O'Shea because he was well aware of her daddy issues, but since he hadn't reached out since he went back to LA, she left well enough alone. Once she got to Alana's house, she walked in, sat down on her sofa, and filled her in on the day's events.

"Damn, that's a trip, but I'm glad you're giving him another chance after all this time, Kels. You know all the drama I've been through with my folks. They get on my nerves, and we definitely don't get along at all, but I love them anyway."

"Me too, and I know it's not going to be easy, but I'm trying to forgive him. It's like when people fuck over me, I have a hard time getting over it. I can hold a grudge like a muthafucka. I guess that's the Aquarius in me. I never thought I would see him again let alone want to build a relationship with him. I think I'm finally growing up, best friend." They both laughed.

"Now if you can forgive him, I think it's about time you forgave O'Shea too. You know you still love that nigga," Alana teased.

"I do, but that's a conversation for another time," she said not ready to talk about her feelings for him yet.

"Enough said, so how is the new job going?"

"Man, I love it, Alana! So much has been going on that I'm just now getting the chance to enjoy it. It's a lot of work, but it's awesome."

"Bitch, we should celebrate. We never really had a chance due to everything that's been going on the last few months. How about next weekend when I'm off? There's this club I've been hearing a lot about that's supposed to be jumping Saturday. All kind of celebrities and ballers be up in there."

"I don't know, Alana. I really don't feel like celebrating," she said sadly. She was missing O'Shea like crazy.

"Fuck that shit, Kelsey. You have to get out of the house. You can't keep moping around waiting on Shea to call. Shit, if you're not willing to tell that man how you feel about him then let's go out and find you another one. He already told you what he wanted. He might just be waiting on you to make the next move." Alana had mad love for O'Shea and wanted nothing more than for her friends to work through their problems and get back together. She had never seen two people who loved each other as much as they did. She felt like they were meant to be.

"Like I said, that's a conversation for another time, Nari Alana Kim."

When Alana heard her government name, she knew Kelsey was serious, so she didn't mention O'Shea again.

"Well, whatever, heifer. Are we going out or what?" she asked changing the subject.

"Fuck it…I'm in!"

"Cool. Next Saturday it's on, bitch" Alana jumped up and started twerking, bouncing her ass cheeks simultaneously as Kelsey laughed. She was cool as fuck and super ghetto. She was a very pretty girl, black and Korean, and reminded Kelsey of the actress Tae Heckard with a much bigger booty. They met in college and ended up working together in the ICU at a local hospital. Alana had always been wild as hell and was the life of the party, so Kelsey was beginning to look forward to kicking it with her bestie next weekend.

After leaving Alana's place, she headed down the hall to her condo and decided to finish up her house cleaning. She had the music blasting as she jammed to old school R&B and cleaned at the same time. The television was on ESPN as usual but was muted as the music played. It was a habit she developed from when she lived with O'Shea that she managed to never let go. As she was dusting around the television, she saw his face appear on the screen. As she muted the music and turned up the volume on the TV, she couldn't believe what she was hearing.

"Free agent O'Shea Lewis signs with Dallas…"

*Shea's playing for the home team now? Damn, this nigga didn't even bother to call and let me know that he was coming back.* What was that shit about?

# Chapter Fourteen

Kelsey and Alana were both dressed to impress as they danced to the Hip Hop music blasting from the speakers in the popular Dallas night club. Her bestie wore a hip hugging white Christian Dior dress with some cute black stilettos, and Kelsey shined in a sleeveless black draped Herve Leger bandage dress with Louboutin Mille Python heels. The two were definitely killing shit, and they knew it. The girls reserved a booth with bottle service and were feeling good and having a great time. Kelsey wanted to reserve a section on the upper level but Alana's dancing-ass just had to be near the dance floor. Off to the right of them was a fine brother scoping Kelsey out, and the longer she looked at him, she recognized that it was Kendrick, the guy she dated in high school before hooking up with O'Shea. He was looking good too but judging from the group of guys he was with, he was still up to the same shit. Kendrick was a dope boy and had been ever since high school. He stood out amongst the others; anyone could tell he was in charge. He still wasn't on a level that she could fuck with though. She figured after all these years, he was still out there on some nickel and dime shit. Kendrick was always the type who let females slow his hustle down. He was more worried about the bitches and wasn't as focused on his bread. Kelsey wasn't above fucking with a nigga like him, but he had to be boss status. She was different like that. She was beautiful and educated, but she was still with that hood shit, and the same went for Alana. Kelsey turned to her girl who was nudging her trying to find out who the dude checking for her friend was.

"Damn, Kelsey, who is that? He ain't took his eyes off you yet."

"Bitch, that's Kendrick. I used to talk to him before I started fucking with Shea."

"Well, bitch, he's fine…don't look now, but he's on his way over here."

"For real?" Kelsey asked, turning around to find Kendrick standing right in front of her.

"What's up, Kelsey? It's been a minute," he said licking his lips.

"Yes, it has. How have you been, Kendrick?"

"I've been straight. I can tell you've been good too, so I won't even bother asking. You still fine as hell, girl," he said flirting with her. He figured that tonight might be his lucky night, and he would finally have a chance with her fine-ass. She was even badder now than she was back in the day.

"Thanks. You don't look too bad yourself," she replied, being polite. He was the same old Kendrick, still running game, and the shit didn't move Kelsey at all.

*Does he not know that I know Trina's his baby mama?* she thought.

He hooked up with her ex-best friend Trina out of spite after she started seeing Shea, and soon after graduation, she became pregnant. She was with child at the same time as his side bitch Cherie. Kelsey had dodged a fucking bullet with that nigga. He continued to talk and she half listened mostly because she couldn't shake the feeling that she was being watched. Her eyes quickly scanned the club after one of Kendrick's potnahs tapped him on the shoulder and whispered something in his ear. Kelsey looked around the club admiring all of the lights when there he was. Seeing him caused her heart to skip a beat and her breathing to pause for a few seconds. O'Shea smiled, and so did she. Kendrick turned his attention back to her and then followed her eyes up to where she was staring, quickly discovering the reason for her smile. He couldn't do shit but laugh.

"I see some things never change," he said shaking his head.

"I'm sorry…what did you say?" Kelsey had not heard a thing he said.

"Nothing…it was good seeing you again, Kelsey," he said before he walked off.

Kelsey didn't bother responding. She didn't have time for him. The man in VIP had her full attention.

"Alana, Shea is here," she told her friend.

"You lying! Where?" Alana asked, looking around trying not to be too obvious.

"Up top," she nodded. Alana looked up and noticed O'Shea staring down at Kelsey.

"Bitch, you on tonight!" They both laughed as Kelsey's phone lit up indicating she had a new text. She smiled as she read his message.

"He wants us to come up to VIP…"

"Shit, let's roll," Alana said excited.

"What about the booth? We spent good money on this shit," Kelsey said.

"Girl, fuck that chump change. Let's see what this VIP do. He might even have some other ballers up there with him. They falling at your feet tonight, hoe, and I'm trying to get on your level, playa," she joked.

The girls laughed as they made their way up to the VIP section where O'Shea and his crew partied. They walked in past all of the thirsty hoes waiting outside the rope trying to get in. The bitches gave them dirty looks, hating on them hard, but they didn't have shit on Kelsey and Alana. Not only were they bad as hell, but they had their own. In life, you need more than just a nice body and a pretty face to get and keep a man. You have to bring something else to the table, and both Kelsey and Alana had their own table.

Although Kelsey was still feeling some type of way about O'Shea not calling her for weeks, she had a great time with him, and the nigga got extra points for looking like a fucking super star. Baby was rocking Versace from head to toe including his cologne and watch. He stood out in a pair of white destroyed jeans paired with a white studded t-shirt and some perforated high-top sneakers. He had those bitches with the Swarovski crystals on them. She loved to see him dressed up, and he knew it. He had all the ladies falling as usual, but he gave her all of his attention, and she loved it. When they weren't dancing, they were chilling and talking. She was in awe of him, and even in Jamaica, she noticed how much he'd grown over the two years they were apart. He was still her Shea but was more mature and had come into the man he was always meant to be. She had changed as well, and she wondered if he dug the new her as much as she was digging the new and improved him.

Alana had caught the eye of O'Shea's college roommate Virgil who currently played for Dallas, and they were getting pretty cozy with one another. Kelsey was glad that she met Alana at the club because she knew her friend was bound to leave with somebody. She was wild like that. Alana Kim did what the fuck she wanted to do with whoever the fuck she wanted to do it with. She was definitely a hot girl. She and Virgil didn't even bother going to breakfast with them after the club was over. Kelsey had known Virgil for years too, so she knew that Alana was in good hands, but she still made her promise to text her later to let her know that she was safe.

After having breakfast, O'Shea and Kelsey sat in the parking lot inside of his Tesla and talked for a while. She was looking good as fuck, and he was having a hard time keeping his eyes off of her in the tight-ass dress she wore. When he spotted her talking to Kendrick in the club, he wanted to go snatch her up, but he could tell she wasn't really feeling anything he was saying, so he chilled.

"I can't believe Kendrick's ass still trying to holla at you after all these years," he said not even attempting to mask his jealousy.

"I know right, and as fine as that nigga is, he still don't have no game, still kicking that whack shit from high school," she laughed.

"So you think that nigga fine, huh?" he asked nodding his head.

"Shut up, Shea," she said, softly punching him in the arm, "Ain't nobody as fine as you though."

"Oh, really?" he asked tossing her a sexy smile as she licked her top lip. *She better quit playing before she gets fucked out here in this parking lot*, he thought to himself.

Kelsey shook her head at the way he was blushing. After a few seconds of silence, she asked the million dollar question. "So, Shea, why haven't you called me since you left? I had to find out on

ESPN of all places that you were coming back to Dallas. What's up with that?"

"To be honest, I wasn't sure where I stood with you. When I left, you had a man, and I didn't want to get in the middle of that. I know you told me what type of relationship you two had, but it seemed that there was more to it. We did our thing in Jamaica, but I didn't want to continue to share you with some other dude. I just figured you would let me know when that was over and you were ready for me." He could tell that by not reaching out, he hurt her feelings, but that was never his intention. He was just trying to give her some space. When he didn't hear from her, he figured she was still seeing Melo, and he was just waiting it out.

"Well, there wasn't more to my relationship with Melo. He wanted more, but I told him that I couldn't give him what he wanted and ended things with him."

"You did? When?" he asked surprised. From what he could tell by watching them at the hospital as well as when he showed up to her place, they were still very much in a relationship.

"Yes, I broke it off with him the day we took Ma home from the hospital. He was pissed, but I just couldn't do it anymore," she shrugged.

"Why didn't you tell me?" He was tripping because the timeline didn't add up. His mother had already been buried the night he showed up to her place unannounced, and it was obvious she and Melo were still messing around.

"I just assumed that you knew because of all the time you and I were spending together. I mean we were together every day, and then you leave, and I don't hear from you again. I knew you were going through a lot, so I didn't want burden you anymore with questions about us."

O'Shea then proceeded to fill her in on his run in with Melo the night he came by to talk to her before going back to LA. He could tell that Kelsey was pissed and surprised by what he was telling her. He recalled how nervous the good doctor was acting that night. He kept looking behind himself as he talked to O'Shea at the door. He now realized that he was afraid she was going to walk out and catch him being petty. O'Shea couldn't believe he let dude play him like that.

"I can't believe that he didn't mention that you stopped by. I should have known something was up when I came out of my room with his shit and he was standing there with his shirt off. I kicked his ass out and threw all of his stuff into the hallway with him. What a fucking creep!"

She was beyond upset. She had been confused and hurt for weeks behind not hearing from O'Shea and come to find out it was all Romelo's doing. Kelsey wished that she would've just followed her heart and continued trying to reach out to O'Shea, but the fear of being rejected held her back. She actually believed that he changed his mind about them being together.

"Hey, all that shit is irrelevant because I'm here now, and it's not by accident. I wanted this trade, so that I could be back here in Dallas with you. You already know how I feel about you, Cocoa Baby. I love you so much, and I want you back. I just need to know what it is you want."

Kelsey closed her eyes and thought back to one of the last conversations she had with Ms. Vickie before she passed away.

*I have to stop being afraid of being hurt and trust in the love I have for this man and the love I know for a fact he has for me.*

She knew in her heart that she didn't want to be without him ever again. These last few weeks had been pure hell, not to mention the two years she spent denying her feelings worried about what others would think of her if she took him back after he cheated. Kelsey never wanted to feel like she was being a fool behind a man. This wasn't just any man though, this was O'Shea, and he was her man. She opened her eyes and looked at him. Holding his gaze, she simply said, "I want you, Shea. I always have and I always will."

"Are you sure because I need you to trust me with your heart again. Never again will I do anything to jeopardize what we have, but I need you to trust that, Kelsey," he said from the heart.

She didn't answer at first but then leaned over and licked his bottom lip before kissing him passionately. "I trust you, O'Shea. I'm all in, baby," she said after pecking him on the lips once more.

"You're staying with me tonight," he said not really giving her a choice.

"Alright, I'll hop in my truck and follow you," she agreed eager for what the night would bring.

\*\*\*

Back at his room at the W hotel, it definitely went down. As soon as they made it across the threshold, it was on.

"Damn, I missed you," he said as he pressed her against the wall, kissing her and palming her round ass.

"I missed you too, Shea."

He pushed her short dress up around her waist and kneeled down until he was face to face with her wet box. He licked and then gently bit down on her clit causing her to moan and scream out his name.

"Tell me you love me, Cocoa," he demanded.

"I love you, Shea," she answered in a shaky voice.

"Again," he said with authority as he inserted two fingers in her pussy. She was dripping wet just like he liked.

"Ohhhh, I love you, Shea," she cried out again as he made love to her with his mouth like only he could, "I love you so much." O'Shea picked her up and took her over to the plush king-size bed. He removed her clothes leaving her naked except for the sexy heels she still had on.

For the rest of the night, they made love like two sex deprived nymphos. Orgasm after orgasm didn't slow them down but instead pushed them to want more and more. By the morning, both sets of Kelsey's lips were swollen and sore from being kissed, sucked, and fucked all night, yet she woke up still wanting more. After a morning soak in the tub and a light breakfast, O'Shea gave her exactly what she craved. They went at it until they couldn't go anymore. When Kelsey woke up again, it was dark outside, and she was still laying on top of him. She remembered riding him until he came and fell asleep, and she fell onto his chest and passed out right after that. His semi-hard dick was still inside of her. When she rose up, he immediately woke up and grabbed her.

"No, don't get up, baby," he pleaded.

"I have to, Shea. I need to get home, babe. I have to go to work in the morning," she protested.

"I'm coming with you then. I don't want to sleep without you tonight," he said planting soft kisses on her neck.

"Ok, baby, how long you planning on staying in this hotel anyway?"

"Just until the house is ready in Preston Hollow."

"Damn, you bought yourself a house already?" she asked surprised.

"No, I bought us a house already. You gone move in when it's ready, right?"

"You want me to move in with you again?"

"Of course I do. I love you, Cocoa."

"I love you too. You need check out of here then. You're coming home with me until the house is ready."

That was music to O'Shea's ears. "Okay, boss lady, let's go home."

# Chapter Fifteen

Months later, Kelsey was having lunch in the cafeteria at work when she ran into Romelo. Surprisingly, she hadn't seen him since she dumped him even though they worked at the same hospital. They weren't enemies, and she really wished him the best, but she was shocked when he actually came over and spoke to her.

"Hey, Kelsey, how have you been?"

"Pretty good, how about you?"

"I've been well." He paused, and then there was an uncomfortable silence. She had no idea what to say. "Hey, I just wanted to apologize to you for how I handled things before. I'll admit that you kept it one hundred with me from the beginning, and then I totally flipped the script on you."

"Thank you for that, but I need to apologize to you too."

"For what?" he asked surprised.

"For the mixed signals. Our relationship was supposed to only be about sex, and then I turned around and brought you around my family. I think I just wanted them to believe I was over my previous situation. I mean, you spent nights at my home like we really dated each other. It wasn't just sex, Romelo. We were in a real relationship, and I'm sorry that I didn't acknowledge it before. I'm also sorry if I hurt you in any way," she said sincerely. Believe it or not, O'Shea was the one who made her realize that she was wrong in the way she handled things with Melo. She didn't want to admit it at first, but she was stringing him along the whole time, and it wasn't right. Although, she was upfront with him about what type of relationship she wanted, when she saw that he wanted more, she should have cut him off then. She knew she was wrong for continuing to play with his feelings when she knew for a fact that nothing would ever come from their relationship.

"Thanks for saying that, Kelsey. You have no idea what that means to me," he replied, "Well, I'm going to take off, but maybe I'll see you around. Take care."

She smiled and nodded. She was glad that they had a chance to clear things up and that there were no ill feelings between them.

***

Later that evening, Kelsey arrived home tired as hell from her long day at work.

"Shea, baby, I'm home," she called out, but he didn't respond. She removed her white coat and hung it up before taking off her shoes in the foyer. "Shea!" she called out again. She knew he was home because his car was in the garage and practice had been over for a while.

*Maybe he's in the shower*, she thought.

When she reached the master bedroom upstairs, the shower wasn't on but there was soft music coming from the bathroom. As she walked in, their garden tub was filled with steaming hot water and bubbles, and there were candles lit all over the place. Her favorite Donny Hathaway CD was playing from the Beats pill on the counter, and there was a note sitting next to it.

*Relax and enjoy your bath. Dinner will be ready when you get out. I Love you, Cocoa.*

*—O'Shea*

Kelsey smiled and removed her work clothes before she slid down into the hot water. She was used to Shea doing things like this for her when they were together before, and she planned to thank him in her own special way later. She stayed in the water until it turned cold. Hopping out of the icy water, she turned on the shower and cleansed her body before lotioning herself down and spraying on her J'Adore by Dior perfume. She dressed in a comfortable heather grey t-shirt dress that O'Shea loved because her ass looked great in it. He was obsessed with her booty, and she knew it. She pulled her curly hair up in a cute messy bun and added some large hoop earrings, NYX Praline butter lip gloss to her lips, and mascara to finish off her simple but cute look.

*My baby went all out,* she thought to herself as she entered the dining room. Shea was there waiting for her, looking good and smelling better as he sat in front of a full spread of delectable foods that filled the large table behind him.

"Hey, beautiful," he said biting his bottom lip. *She knows I love that fucking dress,* he thought.

"Hey, love," she said as she walked over and straddled him, kissing him softly on the lips, "Thank you so much for running me a bath. It was just what I needed. I sure did miss you today."

"Mmm….you can show me just how much you missed me later. Let's have a little dinner first," he said trying to stop their make out session from going any further.

"What if I want to show you now?" she asked licking and kissing on his neck. She felt his dick poking her center. At the moment, she was glad she decided against wearing panties, but he stopped her just as she was reaching for his zipper.

"Kelsey, baby," he said trying to get control of himself, "Come on, let's eat first. I need to talk to you about something anyway."

Her man obviously had something on his mind, so she kissed him on the lips and then got up to fix their plates. "So what's going on, baby?" she asked hoping everything was okay. He was looking too serious which made her nervous. She knew something was up because he never turned down pussy. "Shea, what's up?" she asked again growing impatient.

"You know, Kelsey, I never thought that I would have another chance to be with you, and I just want to thank you for giving us another try. Although, it was hard being away from you these past two years, I believe we needed that time apart so that we could work on ourselves and come back better for each other. I loved you before, but I love you so much more now. This is the happiest I've been in my life, and I don't ever want it to end. I told you I wanted forever, and that's exactly what I'm asking you for," he said as he got down on one knee in front of her. She placed her hand over her heart in shock. She was not expecting this at all. "I love you. I have always loved you, and I promise to love you forever. Will you marry me, Cocoa Baby?" he asked, his face full of emotion. He opened the ring box, and there sat a humongous Tiffany yellow diamond ring. Kelsey wiped the single tear from her face and looked him square in his eyes.

"Of course I'll marry you, O'Shea Ramone Lewis. I love you so much, baby," she answered as they embraced tightly. He proceeded to place the beautiful engagement ring on her finger. After hugging and kissing for a while, he broke away to stand back to his feet and grab her hand.

"Now come back over here and show a nigga how much you missed him today," he said walking her over to his seat at the head of the table. She was more than happy to oblige. They didn't get to eat any of the food on their plates, opting to go upstairs instead after round one in the dining room. They ended up making love all night only pausing to come back downstairs to get some of the good food that sat untouched on the table.

# Epilogue

## 10 Months Later…

"**I** now pronounce you husband and wife. You may kiss your bride," announced Pastor Johnson, bringing the lovely wedding ceremony to an end.

And kiss her he did. O'Shea kissed his bride like it was the very first time. Although, their wedding day was the best day of their lives, it was also bittersweet because Vickie wasn't there to witness their union. O'Shea knew that she was looking down from heaven happy that they finally worked things out. They placed a rose in the chair where she would have sat if she were there as well as one for her brother Kelvin. Alana served as Kelsey's maid of honor, and Virgil acted as best man. For some reason, the two could no longer stand each other but acted like they had some sense for their friends' day. Kelsey was happy that her father was there to walk her down the aisle. They were slowly but surely rebuilding their relationship too. They had dinner a few times each month, and she even attended church with him from time to time. He was very active in the ministry and was going on four years of being clean. Kelsey also believed that her mother and father had started seeing each other again on the low. She came to her mother's house once late at night and found her father's car parked in the driveway. She figured they would tell her what was up when they were ready, but she was glad her mother had someone in her life to make her happy again. It proved to her even more that true love never died.

The wedding was simply beautiful. Tons of friends, family, coworkers, and even a few NBA players and their wives were in attendance. O'Shea held his bride tightly as they danced their first dance as husband and wife.

"Baby, you look so beautiful. I was about to cry like a little bitch when I saw your pretty-ass walking toward me," he whispered in her ear.

"You sure know what to say," she said tilting her head to the side to stare up at her handsome husband.

"Now when you gon' give a nigga some babies? I want about five little chocolate ones who look just like you."

"Ooh, yeah, and I hope they have your dimples." After a short pause, she added, "Well, you might not have to wait as long as you think." Her voice was so low that he almost didn't hear her.

"What did you say?" he asked needing clarification.

"I said you might not have to wait as long as you think. I took a pregnancy test yesterday, and it was positive," she beamed.

At that moment, he couldn't have been any happier. He had his lady back, and now she was going to give him a child.

"Why didn't you tell me, Cocoa?"

"I wanted to go to the doctor to confirm it before I told you, but you know I can't hold water." They both laughed because she told him everything and couldn't keep a secret to save her life.

He was grinning from ear-to-ear as he picked his wife up, spinning her around as everyone looked at them curiously.

"Chill, Shea, we can't say anything until we know for sure."

"I can feel it in my heart, baby, but I'll keep it to myself…for now," he replied as he pulled Kelsey into him and kissed her. She wrapped her arms around his neck, and he sang in her ear, "My Cocoa Baby is about to have my baby…"

"Are you happy, Shea?"

"Happier than I've ever been, and it's all because of you. Thank you for giving me a second chance to love you the right way, Kelsey."

"And thank you for your forever kind of love," she said, kissing her best friend, lover, and soul mate.

**The End**

## Available on Amazon, Barnes & Noble, and Google Play!

**What happens when the Glamorous Life isn't so pretty?**

Calil "Cash" Washington gave up his dreams of doing music to settle down with his longtime girlfriend Nadia Moreaux. After being unfaithful and being caught up in his fame, he refocuses his energy on being a better man for her, but after getting a 9-5, he quickly realizes that the square life is just not for him. Music is in his blood. There was no denying it, but Nadia wasn't ready to let him go again until she realized that she had dreams of her own too.

After hooking up with one of the hottest female rappers in the Bay Area, Lexx Gang, Cash is ready to spread his musical wings. Trying to balance two different lives, he must ultimately face the consequences when someone close to him loses their life because of it all. Will Cash and Nadia make it out of all the flashing lights in one piece, or will the cold City nights send them back where they came from with nothing?

With non-stop drama, action, and revenge, City Nights will have you on the edge of your seat until the very last page.

www.blackedenpublications.com

**Available on Amazon, Barnes & Noble, and Google Play!**

Jasmine Young was head over heels in love with her boyfriend of four years, Tarrell Coleman—or so she thought until she caught him in bed with another woman in the home they shared together. Finally finding the nerve to take her independence back, Jasmine decides to get a place of her own with her best friend Chantae to get away from all the drama.

Over the course of trying to get over Tarrell, Jasmine quickly develops a friendship with June Robertson. The two connect instantly, and after one fateful night, she realizes that he's the one who's been there all along and not Tarrell. Ready to take a chance on "true" love, Jasmine abandons all of her relationships and principles and falls fast into June's arms, but will he be there to catch her, or will she be left standing alone to pick up all the pieces?

www.blackedenpublications.com

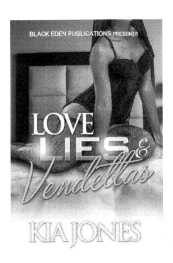

## Available on Amazon, Barnes & Noble, and Google Play!

What does a beautiful cop and a handsome, smooth-talking king pin have in common? Love...

For years Tyrone "Ty" Gibbs was the king of Dallas. He had everything he could ever wanted in life—until things suddenly took a turn for the worse. Friends turned sour, his homeboy was murdered, and his side chick jumps ship. Ty took his licks like a man, but makes a promise that everyone will ultimately pay in the end.

Dixon was supposed to be undercover as she single-handedly worked to take down Ty's empire, but there was one problem. She didn't expect to fall in love with him along the way. Misty wasn't just a side chick to Ty. She was also his down fall until she fled and was never to be seen again...or so people thought.

Filled with secrets, betrayal, and a mind-blowing twist, "Love, Lies, and Vendettas" is sure to take you on a wild and riveting ride.

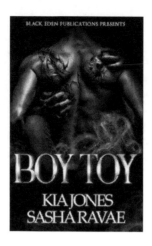

**Available on Amazon, Barnes & Noble, and Google Play!**

Don Crip was recently released from prison with nothing but a chip on his shoulder. All he longed for was to find his baby mother and to make things right again, but, there's one problem...she's now married!

His best friend, Pierre, is the total opposite. Though he is in love with his on-again off-again girlfriend, Malaysia, he can't seem to keep his hands off of her friends. Being that Malaysia is married with three kids, you would think that it would be easy for him to walk away, but it's not.

Will Don Crip and Pierre find their way through the battle field of love or should they watch what they ask for?

# FREE! FREE! FREE!

Reagan Taylor's life as a basketball wife isn't as perfect as she expected. After enduring an abusive relationship for over seven years, she meets the man of her dreams. Her eyes are finally opened to true love for the first time, but will it last? Jewel Sanchez, a self-made d-boy, hustles every day to provide himself with the life he has been accustomed to since birth. As lieutenant of the M.A.C. Boys, Jewel makes sure he keeps his money close and soon his enemies closer. Robyn Johnson, a rich, party girl, is known all over Sacramento, but maybe for the wrong reasons. She often attempts to medicate herself with material objects and different men, but the pain never goes away. She was always proud of her strength, but will that be enough for her to survive? Brandon Edwards' short-fuse proves to be dangerous for everyone around him. Always use to getting what he wants, Brandon does whatever it takes to hold onto his power and respect even if that means losing a few people along the way.

**Available on Amazon, Barnes & Noble, and Google Play!**
www.blackedenpublications.com

BLACK EDEN PUBLICATIONS

## *Please send order form to:*

*Black Eden Publications, LLC*
*P.O. Box 3375, Hayward, CA  94540*
*info@blackedenpublications.com*

**Thank you for your order!**

**Shipping  Information:**

Date: _____

Name: _____

Address: _____

Email: _____ (Optional)

City/State/Zip: _____  _____  _____

**Pricing:**

    a.   Shipping + $3.00
    b.   Receive a 15% discount when you order **5
    or more books** during the same order.

| Title | Price | # of Books | Total |
|-------|-------|-----------|-------|
| Boy Toy | $15.00 | | $ |
| City Nights | $15.00 | | $ |
| Cocoa Baby | $15.00 | | $ |
| Counterfeit Dreams | $15.00 | | $ |
| Counterfeit Dreams 2: A Hustler's Hope | $15.00 | | $ |
| Counterfeit Dreams 3: A Dream's Nightmare | $15.00 | | $ |
| Counterfeit Dreams 4: A Dream's Nightmare | $15.00 | | $ |
| Counterfeit Dreams: The Complete Collection | $40.00 | | $ |
| Disciple in America: A Teenage Guide to Faith | $10.00 | | $ |

*"Welcome to the Inner Circle..."*

| | | | |
|---|---|---|---|
| Dying for Change | $15.00 | | $ |
| Freaky's World | $15.00 | | $ |
| Love, Lies, and Vendettas | $15.00 | | $ |
| Love, Lies, and Vendettas 2 | $15.00 | | $ |
| Ski Mask Divas | $15.00 | | $ |
| Trap Goddess | $15.00 | | $ |
| What Bae Don't Know | $15.00 | | $ |

**Payment** (Check appropriate box):

- ☐ Money Order
- ☐ Check
- ☐ Pay Using Credit Card (Please contact info@blackedenpublications.com for invoice)

*"Welcome to the Inner Circle..."*

Made in the USA
San Bernardino, CA
28 February 2016